Also, by Tre LaVin:

Thank God At Rock Bottom, Jesus Was The Rock That I Hit!

Clutching Bricks: Poetry Without Apologies

PLIGHT
OF THE
FORTUNATE

Tre LaVin

authorHOUSE

AuthorHouse™
1663 Liberty Drive
Bloomington, IN 47403
www.authorhouse.com
Phone: 833-262-8899

© 2021 Tre LaVin. All rights reserved.

No part of this book may be reproduced, stored in a retrieval system, or transmitted by any means without the written permission of the author.

This is a work of fiction. All of the characters, names, incidents, organizations, and dialogue in this novel are either the products of the author's imagination or are used fictitiously.

Published by AuthorHouse   04/27/2021

ISBN: 978-1-6655-2422-3 (sc)
ISBN: 978-1-6655-2423-0 (hc)
ISBN: 978-1-6655-2424-7 (e)

Library of Congress Control Number: 2021908491

Print information available on the last page.

Any people depicted in stock imagery provided by Getty Images are models, and such images are being used for illustrative purposes only.
Certain stock imagery © Getty Images.

This book is printed on acid-free paper.

Because of the dynamic nature of the Internet, any web addresses or links contained in this book may have changed since publication and may no longer be valid. The views expressed in this work are solely those of the author and do not necessarily reflect the views of the publisher, and the publisher hereby disclaims any responsibility for them.

Oh, to be special in that particular way...elevating from the surface of what they heard and leaving them to wallow in the depths of what they can never even begin to understand...

This work is dedicated to all who are struggling to balance what others see against what it is yet to be conceived in an effort to do more than just merely exist.

Contents

Introduction ix

Chapter 1	Congress Park	1
Chapter 2	The Other Twin's Best Friend	11
Chapter 3	New Dimensions	23
Chapter 4	The Seed of Disruption	33
Chapter 5	16	43
Chapter 6	Impactful Decisions	51
Chapter 7	Profiles in Courage	63
Chapter 8	Quicksand	75
Chapter 9	Limping to the Finish	85
Chapter 10	Trial For Error	97
Chapter 11	College Bound, Trouble Found	107
Chapter 12	It All Comes Down to This	117

About the Author 127

Introduction

Where to even begin? All my life I've heard that if I just continue moving forward there will be no reason to look back. Doing everything the way I'm supposed to in order to meet everyone else's expectations has its benefits, but I am not a robot either. I know we just met but let me show you where I am, or better yet, let me introduce you to my deeper thoughts through one of my many journal entries:

Addiction
He didn't know that he had it
This thing called a habit
He liked the fact that he could love it
So much that he hid his lust for it
They courted for awhile
Seeing each other in passing
Three weeks was all it took
To get to know his friend called Passion
Whenever they got together
He was totally free
They would meet on weekends
At the corner of distortion and reality
Taking a detour from responsibility
Always trying to capture missing priorities
They closed so many doors throwing away the key
That his own mirror
Couldn't stand the fractured sight of he
In gaining one friend
He pushed the others away

Until, finally, he and Passion
Saw each other what seemed like everyday
After about six months
He couldn't recognize
The man he had become,
Whom so many would despise
Many people tried to tell him
But he just wouldn't listen
He couldn't bring himself to see
His friend Passion, as an addiction

So, there's that…but why even talk to you? No one else seems to be listening or let alone, care. Sometimes speaking in third person helps me to create some distance between where I've been, where I am, and where I'm going. Quite honestly, from moment to moment I am not always entirely sure where that is even supposed to be. In trying to forge my own path it feels like I have never been able to escape this lingering shadow. Let me tell you, the weight of that has been suffocating at times. Telling you where I am is easy enough…showing you just how I got here, now **that** is a different story…

One

Congress Park

Confidence brings conviction to conversation. All my life I have heard some version of this same phrase. It is my father's way of saying that belief in oneself coupled with the audacity and courage to stand for up for it will give anyone the tools needed to express themselves to others and be heard. I remember thinking once how much being heard was important but then challenging myself to find a more impactful way to make sure that I, Gabriel Clarkson, could be understood.

I have always known that I was here on this earth to do more than just exist. The trouble was that everyone (my parents especially) just **expected** that I would just do what was right. A solid reputation is a great thing to have, and I DO have one, don't get me wrong...but I also have vices...you know, shortcomings. I am tainted and imperfect and I do struggle from time to time or moment to moment. Yet, whenever I mention such things, I am told to just shake them off and keep pushing forward because the best is still to come.

I have been going off script for a while, in my head at least trying to hold fast to the belief that the greatness that my father has proclaimed for me will come to pass. I certainly don't want to let him down because Andrew Clarkson is NOT someone that you let down! But the pressure to not fail at times has overrode the pressure to succeed and be the best that I could be. Those things may sound like they are the same but trust me when I tell you they are not!

TRE LaVIN

One of the hardest parts of the self-serving identify crisis that I now find myself in stems from what I see when I look in the mirror because I don't just see my father but also my twin sister, Delila. We may come from the same gene pool, but that mirror shows me the parts of myself I can't run from and the other parts of me that I should embrace but have not yet built up the courage to explore, those parts of my inadequacy that Delila seems to have mastered.

Perceptions can get clouded. I've run into people who seem to think that just because I am well spoken or carry myself a certain way that I somehow got everything handed to me. My mother, Sophie has a saying: "Everything earned, nothing given!" Now my mother and sister get typecast all the time by people thinking that there is no brain attached to the natural outer beauty that they possess. That is until someone crosses them or makes the wrong assumption. At that point, all who confidently strode over struggle back carrying the dropped jaws of their misconceptions with them like a ball and chain. My mother has a term she uses to describe such people, often saying that those with these types of misgivings can't help it if they are *stuck stiff*.

I have a good life. I won't deny that, nor should I. I have been a straight A student all throughout high school and am now set to be the salutatorian of my college graduating class. I grew up in church. In all honesty though I have reached a point where there seem to be more questions than answers regarding the way I should be walking on this spiritual journey. Just because mom and dad said it and grandma prayed for it, does that make it all right? I am beginning to wonder.

This brings me back to my father. He is what some people would call a self-made man. He can't stand excuses, so he makes none and refuses to allow his family to become stagnant to the point where we either make excuses or worse, become one. If there is ever a problem, he likes to solve it by walking out one of his many sayings, (called Drew-isms by those who know him best): *the solution is in the soil*. We all take this to mean that we can't grow if we are not willing to dig deep and turn over a few rocks.

Ever since I was little, I always looked up to my father. He is my hero. He has always given me the confidence to know that if the work is done right the reward will show up in the results. I've seen this man endure, persevere, overcome, and ultimately win. He is a pillar in our community, one who has done all he could to lay the groundwork for the legacy that he hopes will be carried forward long after he is gone. My sister and I are aware of what he and my mother have sacrificed for us and the responsibility we have going forward to make our own mark as we are tasked to not only preserve the legacy but carry it forward leaving it even better than we found it.

We are not from the gutter and quite honestly, I don't know what it means to go *without,* but I DO know what it means to have to *work* for everything I have. Delia and I were taught early to respect others and take nothing for granted. At the same time, we were taught to be prepared and not to be intimidated walking into any room. It is our job to enter a room full of questions and walk out leaving only the assurance of definitive answers.

Denver, Colorado has shaped and molded the man I have become. I am proud to be from here. There is something uniquely special about the "Mile High City" as it has become known, gaining its name from the fact that the city sits one mile above sea level. My parents are from here. My dad graduated from Manual High, and my mom graduated from George Washington High in the city. They met in college at the University of Denver, or DU as we Denverites call it, after earning basketball scholarships, with dad studying law and mom studying art history. Dad would later earn his Juris Doctor (JD) from DU as well. He is now a prominent lawyer in the city, having started his own practice, the Clarkson Firm, and mom is an art history professor at DU.

Delila is full of confidence. While we were in middle school, she was introduced to theatre arts and she was instantly hooked. Ever since that first encounter, life has always been a stage. I am proud of my sister. She has really found an outward channel that allows her the freedom of expression. For college she decided to go to DU, following our parents and continuing the Pioneer legacy.

We are people who love sports, food, and the arts. It is not uncommon to find a member of the Clarkson family somewhere in the city at a Broncos, Nuggets, Rockies, or Avalanche game. You are just as likely to find us at the Denver Art Museum or Fillmore Auditorium showing an appreciation for art and live music. We have a running joke in the family that captures the spirit of our family to the core. See, Fillmore Auditorium is located on Clarkson Street and dad likes to think that we are meant to be there given that our family name and the street that the auditorium sits on are one in the same.

All those places are wonderful, but I always find the most serenity at nearby Ferril Lake, located in City Park, which is just under a mile from the family home. Growing up, whenever I was stressed and needed to clear my head I would go to the lake, sit in the park, and write. A sunset glistening off the lake is one of the more beautiful sights I have ever seen in my lifetime.

Why do I find so much peace there? There are two reasons, nature doesn't ask for much and blank pages of loose-leaf paper don't talk back. Delila and I have this saying, "D has her stage and G has his page." When one of us mentions this, the other already knows that there is a real need to process whatever we are dealing with and the places that we do this allow us the freedom to find ourselves before we got lost completely.

On another note, growing up in the Baptist Church has been a great experience for our family as well. My entire spiritual journey has been cultivated at Zion Baptist Church, which also happens to be the oldest church in the Rocky Mountain western region, having been established back in 1865. The church is located just under two miles from our home and less than a mile from where dad grew up. Some of my greatest memories and moments have happened in and around that place.

Dad also made sure that Sundays were free for church, Broncos games in football season, and mom's Sunday dinners. Mom's lamb chops with roasted red potatoes and asparagus along with her smothered pork chops with mac and cheese, collard greens, and cornbread are mainstays that are always requested. Those dinners eventually took on a life of their own as it was not uncommon to see any and everybody in the neighborhood stop through after church to grab a bite to eat, watch the game, and listen to some good music. Mom and dad's favorite musical group is Earth, Wind, and Fire with the songs "September," "Shining Star," and "Reasons" serving as family favorites.

If we weren't inside, we were out on the basketball court in the back yard. The games of one on one were always intense but those were nothing compared to the fierce two on two games we would play as a family. The only person I ever met that was more intense that my father when it came to sports was my mother. That mentality carries over into everything the Clarksons do, and it shows. Spades. Dominoes. Darts. The game itself doesn't matter but there must be a winner because mom doesn't believe in playing if you can't keep score.

It has always been important to my parents that Delila and I have a deep sense of community and they have not only encouraged us to make a positive impact where we live but also have been a wonderful example of what that looks like. It didn't matter if we were volunteering at the food bank, handing out socks to the homeless, or serving food at the local soup kitchen, the goal was always to have their children know that one wrong choice or bad break could instantly change not only our fortunes but also our circumstances.

They also made sure to let us know the value of hard work. "Just because we have made a little money Gabriel, doesn't mean that we shouldn't cut our own yard" I remember dad telling me once. He and mom let us know the importance of being able to make money for ourselves. "Gabriel and Delila whenever you get something as a result of making your own money, you will always appreciate more," mom would tell both of us often, so much so that we could finish that sentence well before she did.

The one thing that is most important to me is *family*. No matter what is going on around me I can always insulate myself in and around them. The highs, the lows, and all the in between. Somewhere in the midst you come to find out who you really have in your corner. The Clarkson family really are down like four flats! When it gets tight Delia likes to say, "Come right or take flight!" We come hard behind the fam. I can't remember a time when our family didn't have each other's back. We all know that depending on the situation our family may be all we have.

I grew up in the Congress Park section of Denver on North

TRE LaVIN

Fillmore Street between East Colfax Avenue and 14th Street. Our neighborhood has the boundaries of York Street to the west, Colorado Boulevard to the east and 6th Avenue to the south. The Denver Botanic Gardens and the East 7th Avenue Historic District are also nearby.

Whether getting the best cuts of meat down at Oliver's, Mexican food from Benny's, Italian food from Borolo Grill or Luca, or BBQ from Kitchen Table there are wonderful restaurants. Catching a movie at Esquire Theatre or a concert in the summer at the Gardens is a unique experience all its own. You can also get good music down at Twist and Shout and a good book down at the Tattered Cover Bookstore.

In this multi-ethnic neighborhood Delila and I made all types of friends, be it White, Latino, Asian, African American, or otherwise. Having such a diverse group of friends allowed us to gain a high level of respect for all people and cultures. Sundays may have been reserved for the Clarksons with mom's Sunday dinners but during the rest of the week you wouldn't be surprised to see any of us at any number of places up and down our block.

This area used to be called "Cemetery Hill." Dad is very aware of this and makes sure to remind all of us that we are not here to simply die but to live a life worthy of humble recognition where God gets ALL the praise. Another saying that dad has popularized goes something like this, "Give all you got before you go six feet down in the plot." As corny as we all know this to sound (and we have told him as much) the foundation that this sits on is the truth itself.

Which leads me to this, which my mother says often, "There are three levels of truth...the one they know, the one you know, and the one they tell." It is mom's way of reminding us to remain true to who we are and *whose* we are, no matter what is surrounding us. Gossip has many friends but the truth itself will walk alone.

I want to let you in and tell my truth. But before I do, I just want you all to understand that there is absolutely no way I can tell this story without painting the clear and proper picture of the place that has set such a firm foundation on which I am forever grateful to stand. The only problem is that as I come back here for spring break, a mere five weeks from my college graduation that firm foundation just may be ready to crumble!

In attempting to leave a legacy apart from my father I am struggling to find out just who I can trust outside of my family. From where I stand, it seems as though everyone I have encountered either has a hand up or a handout. I must confess that if you're not willing to match my energy I can't rock with you. With everything I've been taught I can ill-afford to let someone ride my coattails to success.

With that said, I am actively re-evaluating exactly what success looks like for me. Many of my friends and contemporaries seem to have figured out quick ways to get where they want to go. It's like they have an instant recipe that only requires that they add water, whereas I'm stuck mixing everything by hand without the aid of an electric mixer and I keep getting chalky lumps rather than a smooth pour.

This process has been wearing me out for quite a while. The vision that I have and what I want to do is crystal clear; it's the method in which to get there that continues to give me a continued source of heartburn. "Hey Gabriel, what are you going to do when you graduate?" is the question that I have been asked a lot lately. Some think I should go work for my father. Others have offered that I should start my own blog and build on my journalism pedigree. Those are solid options, but I want to make a deeper impact.

So, what to do then? I want to start a 501 c 3 nonprofit that will equip the next generation with the skills necessary to write and express themselves in a safe and engaging manner, one that not only will challenge them to think independently but also show them the value of collaboration in an effort to build something bigger than them. I want them to start when they are sixth graders and build a bridge not only for high school but college and beyond. As a lover of words, it just seems like a natural fit.

Going to school in Boulder, Colorado at the University of Colorado, Boulder (CU) has been gratifying for me. Boulder is about 25 miles north of Denver and is a beautiful college town with a lot going for it. Be that as it were, I really want to birth this nonprofit in my neighborhood and give something back to my city as a thank you for all that the city has given to me. I know that doing so would not only be a great source of pride for me, but it would be the surest way to pay back my parents for all they have instilled in me.

This endeavor probably would not be so difficult but for the pressure that I put on myself. I don't want to come up short because to come up short will mean that I failed. Failure means letting myself, my family, and especially my father down and I already told you that letting Andrew Clarkson down cannot be on my list of to-dos.

I want my parents to have the ultimate confidence that I can handle this huge undertaking. Yet this is much easier said than done because I know that I must have an answer, a way out, and a way forward for each scenario that mom and dad will present. To make matters worse, Delila has already presented her purpose, plan, and portfolio to our parents and received their blessing. Knowing that she has already withstood the pressure from the firing squad, she too is breathing down my neck wanting to know not what I will do but how I will get it done.

I am acutely aware of the shift going on within myself. Rather than stumble upon words in real time responding to questions from others that would have put me on the defensive, I turned to the one entity that I knew would not judge, and more importantly would fully understand: my pen and that loose-leaf...

Transitions
I've been going through the subtlety of artful changes
Making unpretentious moves of transcendence, rites of passage
Transformations that reflect a shift and conversion
That can only be explained by experiences in how I function
Adjustments rooted in the tilled and fertilized soil of adaptation
Life lessons provided water to seeds of immaturity that made me sick
Altering appearance and character through circumstance, a metamorphosis
As I continued to grow, I made a choice to flip darkness with light's switch
Walking through process on the path of evolution,
leaving the Master's footprint

PLIGHT OF THE FORTUNATE

Even writing this in 2021, I am wrestling with morality and the integrity, or lack thereof, associated with the central virtue of its principles. Flipping that switch from darkness to light has left me to try to steady myself while walking a tightrope of indecision while my emotions are wrought with the precariousness of almost certain peril. I am certain that I cannot let those closest to me know the depth of what I have been left to process because the prospects of what lay ahead and the fact that I am even considering such things would render me completely unrecognizable, in theory anyway...

So, let me take you back down my lane full of great memories and introduce you to some more of the important people that I built those special times with. Each piece of this complicated puzzle that I now see got its origin back around the time I started high school. No doubt, the benchmark moments that I now recall stand as an intricately woven piece that now constructs the fabric of my being. Even as I am beginning to fray at the seams there is still a solid foundational core that is fighting to hold me together...

Two

The Other Twin's Best Friend

"**G**AB-RI-EEEEEL!" Delila was screaming at me from down the street. Startled, I managed a weak, "What up Twin?" Delila was absolutely beside herself. "He asked me! He asked me!" Now I was confused. "Who is he and what did he ask?" I wanted to know. "Devin Palmer asked me to the Homecoming Dance, and I told him I wanted to go" she went on to say, by this point completely out of breath. Devin is a good friend of the family who we met in church. He and his family live on the next block over on Detroit Street. Devin and I have been tight going all the way back to 6th grade when he first moved here from California. To say that Delila has a crush on him would be an understatement. She has been trying to get his attention for years. I guess getting his attention got a lot easier once she grew a fully developed chest over the summer. Now as we entered our Freshman year of high school the social landscape as we knew it was changing.

The year is 2013 and a little more than one month into the school year my voice has finally found its deep range and girls who were paying me no attention when the last school year ended suddenly were dropping me notes trying to get my phone number. I didn't mind the attention, but I knew my mom might have a thing or two to say about it. Her voice was never far from my conscience, "Gabriel make sure you respect these girls and show them how a gentleman is supposed to act. Open doors for them, pull out chairs, and be actively engaged in conversation so that they know that you have a genuine interest in who they are and not just what they can do," she would always tell me.

She did not know this yet, but mom didn't have to worry about all these different girls keeping my attention because there was only one that I had any interest in. Gina Richardson had been Delila's bestie since 4th grade and lived three houses down from us. Her mom, like ours is a professor at DU and her dad is the head basketball coach at Thomas Jefferson High. Gina and I can talk about anything and we have over the years. She is a huge tomboy who has never been afraid to speak her mind or mix it up. I'm still mad that she is better than me at NBA 2K, but I take the cake in Madden.

Delila had her date for the dance but I was still hoping that I might ask Gina to go with me. I wasn't sure if she already had a date though and my confidence would be destroyed if I were to ask, and she shot me down. So, I waited. But now there are less than two weeks to the big day, so I have asked my sister to do some detective work for me. You would think I would already know if she had a date, but I honestly didn't and now the curiosity was beginning to be too much. I had been waiting on a text from Delila to tell me what I needed to know but I hadn't gotten it before she came screaming at me from down the street. She would apologize for getting sidetracked thinking that the sheepish grin on her face would save her.

Finally, at 6:45 pm my text would come. "Make your move Bro," the text read, "but make it soon because she has a couple of boys who may ask her before the weekend." As I read this, I couldn't help but think, "Damn, its already Thursday night, I am running out of time." I dialed Gina's number, but she didn't pick up. We would be eating dinner at 7 and I wanted to hurry so I told D to hold it down for me until I got back. "I got you G, but you know I can't hold dad off for too long," she told me as I rushed out the door.

I hopped the fence at Gina's and knocked on her bedroom window. She motioned for me to come around and come inside. "Sorry I missed your call Gabe, I was on the phone with my dad, what's up?" she asked as she greeted me at the door. At this point a bout of extreme nervousness came over me. As much as

I had talked to Gina about some of everything over the years this should not have been hard, but the cat got my tongue. I opened my mouth trying to force words that wouldn't come. Finally, I stammered, "Umm, so Gina, I...I..." The look on Gina's face changed from one of happiness to one of deep concern, "Gabe, are you okay, what's wrong, you have me worried now, what's going on?" A few more seconds would pass before I finally got it out, "Gina I know we have always been cool and its no big deal really, but I was wondering if you would go with me to Homecoming?" She started blushing immediately, "Dang Gabe, you like me like *that*? What did I miss? I always thought I was just your home girl..."

"Well, you *are*...my home girl but honestly I think it would be cool if we tried this thing together, I mean if it's cool with you," I said sounding more awkward with each passing word. "But, if you don't want to, I..." Gina cut me off, "Boy what am I going to say to that? Yeah, it's cool. I would love to go with you." Gina never fancied herself as even remotely cute, but she was fine for real. Sounding unsure of herself she asked, "Gabe do you think I'm pretty?" As I answered this question, I was sure of that much, saying, "Hell yeah, but I never said anything because we were always out on a court or something, so I guess it never came up, but yeah, I think you are beautiful." I continued, "What you don't think so?" Her answer surprised me. "No, I don't but it really helps to know that you think so. Thanks."

I had been at Gina's house for less than five minutes but in that moment time stood still. "Well, I got to get home, dinner is ready, and you know my dad doesn't play when it's time to eat," I said as I turned to leave. There was a tear in Gina's eye, "Gabe this is embarrassing to say but I don't have anything to wear for the dance." I told her not to worry, we would figure something out and make sure that she would feel as beautiful on that night as I have always known her to be. "See ya later," Gina said as I hopped the fence to return home.

As I made it back home dad was calling me for dinner, "Gabriel, I know you hear me, Son, we *will* start without you." Delila had covered for me, saying, "Daddy Gabe was checking the mailbox for me because I forgot. Sorry." As I kissed mom, I could see D mouthing, "Is everything cool? How did it go? Is your pride still intact?" She was messing with me now. "Later, I'll catch you up after we eat," I told her not wanting to say much right then because I still couldn't believe what just happened. But my mom cut right through me and got right down to it.

"Dang Son, you left here in a hurry and came back blushing. What's her name?" she would ask. "Mom, it's not one of the girls you are probably thinking but I do have a date for the dance," I said as my confidence began to rise. "Well, Gabe, who is it?" dad asked me impatiently. I couldn't talk. "C'mon Twin is it who I texted you about of what???" D wanted to know. "Well, umm, I asked Gina and she accepted," I answered. Dad looked surprised, "Ok, then. I always knew y'all were cool, but I didn't know you were sweet on her like *that*! Well done, very well done." Mom would interject next, telling dad, "So, Andrew, Gabe isn't the only one who got a date for Homecoming!" Dad was beaming now. "Okay baby girl, who you got?" Delila couldn't contain her excitement, "Well daddy Devin asked me today! I'm so excited! I really like him! A LOT!"

Mom was starting to cry. "Look at my babies getting all grown on me now," she said managing to crack a smile. "Delila we are going to have so much fun getting you ready, I can't wait," mom said as she got up to hug my sister. Dad extended his arm across the table to me and as he dapped me up, he let out a strong, "My dude!" We had just sat down at the table to have pizza and then mom flipped the entire mood. With a bit of a quizzical look on her face she said, "Hmmm if I would have known all this was going to happen, I would have made something a little more formal to celebrate..." As we all started laughing, Delila said, "It's all good mom, it really is."

As Delila and I finished eating we let out a big "I see you Twin," in unison. I said, "If I would've known that we were going to have this happen to both of us today, I wouldn't have waited so long." As D shook her head in agreement, I told her, "Thank you watchdog, I really owe you for this one." Delila's look turned to surprise, "Bro I didn't know you were sweet on Gina like that though, I guess we both had to get it going with the Twin's best friend, huh?" "D, you stupid," I cracked, "but you are right. Who knew?"

As D and I were chilling outside, Devin and Gina came walking up asking us if we wanted to hoop. Of course, my sister and I were game but with all that had transpired this 2 on 2 battle took on a different meaning. As the game got deeper it didn't take long for our collective competitive streaks to take over. Gina and I would win after I sent Devin's shot right back in his face and put the next shot off the backboard and through the hoop. We didn't know it at the time, but that night was the first of many that the four of us would spend together going forward.

Going to school the next day felt different. It seemed that I had more responsibility regarding Gina now. I always listened to what my mother told me about how to act around girls but now I wanted to prove to her that I was paying attention. We had the same lunch period, so I made sure to catch up with her. I wasn't having second thoughts about the dance and I was hoping that she wasn't either. I've heard about how going out with somebody can change the dynamics of a friendship and I didn't want the fact that Gina and I had a cool vibe to change. "Am I overthinking this," I began to wonder. After all it wasn't like Gina was my girlfriend or anything like that but now that we are going to this dance together, I was beginning to look at her differently.

Devin hit me up before 5th period. "Yo, G, your sister said yes, man!" Knowing that D already let me know this, I played it cool. "Yeah Dev, she may have mentioned something about that," I said, unable to hold contain my laughter. "I'm going to be watching you though Dev...don't even think about hurting my sister, she really likes you," I let him know in a stern voice and with the straightest of faces so he would know how serious I was. In response Devin's voice was reassuring, "Gabe, I know you don't play behind your sister, we cool, I really like her too." Now that we had that understanding, I went on with the rest of my day.

In algebra class though my mind kept wandering back to Gina. I just wanted to do right by her and show her a good time. Not that I had to impress her, but I really wanted to do the best I could to make Homecoming a special night for the both of us but especially for her. "Ouch, what was that for?" I said as I turned around to Delila sitting behind me. As she hit me again, she said, "You MUST get out of la-la land big head, you're daydreaming. It's your turn up at the board. Question 3."

Now Mr. Jackson our algebra teacher was calling me. "Gabriel, please give the class your answer for question 3 and don't forget to show your work." "No problem sir," I said, trying to regain my focus. Delila cut her eyes at me as only she could and mouthed, "Damn Bro, that was close." Dad told me that girls could have your nose open. Now for the first time I was starting to see exactly what he meant. Delila, on the other hand, was certain that she and Devin were meant to be. There was absolutely no doubt in her mind, as evidenced by the hearts and smiley faces she was doodling in her notebook while she was supposed to be taking notes. "I guess I'm not the only one with a head in the clouds," I said, rolling my eyes at her. My eye roll was met with a swift kick in the shin and a smile you could see from here to the city of Aurora. Truth be told, I was extremely excited for the both of us. It is always a good thing to see my sister happy.

My sister talked to mom about Gina not having anything to wear for the dance and my mom came up with an idea. Mom, Delila, and Mrs. Richardson, Gina's mom, went to one of the bridal boutiques in town and got the girls dresses. My dad saw pictures of the dresses and said there was no way that I was going to look busted on Homecoming night, so we went searching for tuxedo rentals too. Once it was confirmed what I would be wearing to the dance, my nerves left.

When the day finally came, dad made sure that we were going to be riding in style. He rented a limousine for the four of us and had it parked out front waiting to take us to the venue. But before we could do that, he sent me to go meet Gina at her house to pick her up and walk her and her parents back to our house for pictures. Devin had already arrived with his parents, so we were just waiting on Delila to come downstairs. Mom was not going to miss an opportunity to have her baby girl make a grand entrance.

The dress that Gina was wearing was nice! She managed to get a strapless blue floor length gown with rhinestones that brought out the hidden sparkle in her eyes. I was trying to contain my excitement knowing that I was going to have the flyest girl in the room once we arrived. I hadn't seen my sister's dress, so I was just as anxious as Devin to see what she was wearing. Sis was rocking this peach and cream number with a choker that instantly reminded me that my brother radar was going to have to be up all night because Delia strode down those steps owning her moment!

All the parents made sure to get a lot of pictures and everyone was all smiles for the cameras. It was cool to be able to get all of us together like this for something more than just ball or cards. As Gina took my hand she whispered, "Gabe thank you so much for even asking me to go. When I didn't think I would have a date this whole thing didn't matter much." In response I told her, "It's cool, you don't know how relieved and glad I was that you actually said yes." Delia said, "Gina you and Gabriel look amazing together," to which Gina responded, "Girl, thanks but you know you and Devin look pretty fly yourselves." Delila being Delila, couldn't resist, "I know that's right, girl, you better tell the truth!" Devin just shook his head as he asked me, "Yo, G has your sis always been *this* vain?" Behind a full on laugh I deadpanned, "From the womb, bro, from the womb!" The entire house was washed in laughter as we made it outside to the limo.

As we headed to the venue the excitement was palpable. None of us really knew what to expect but we couldn't wait to find out either. When we arrived, we fellas went around to let the ladies out and when they stood up, whew, I had goosebumps. When I looked at Gina and then at my sister, I realized just how lucky I was to be present in that moment. To be a part of that was next level for me. It's weird to realize that at the age of 14. I just wanted to bottle that moment. I was also able to spend that time with my best friend too. To that point in my life, I hadn't felt anything better than that! The best part of it though is that the night would only get better.

Once we got inside, we chopped it up with some of our other friends, had some snacks, and cracked so many jokes. I don't remember laughing so much talking about absolutely nothing! I stole a moment just gazing into Gina's eyes. The smile on her face was so real and true. During one of the slow dances as she laid her head on my chest, I could feel her heartbeat and it's like we were in perfect sync. I looked over at Devin and watched him as he looked into Delila's eyes and it was just *different*...my twin looked like she was on cloud nine! With the four of us in that moment I got a snapshot of what true happiness can look like.

My parents have a unique kind of love story and being there with my friends and with my sister allowed me to see the depth of beauty that can come from getting to know somebody and growing together with them. That night at Homecoming I saw something and felt something even more. I saw and felt what it meant to be a part of something that was bigger than myself, to build a foundation worth standing on with people that I care about and who genuinely care about me.

When we all got back to Congress Park after the dance the four of us decided to take a walk around City Park. A slight breeze accompanied us as we all passed next to Ferril Lake. We could see the Rocky Mountains far off in the distance and the moon lit the water and provided a perfect backdrop to capture the final moments of the night. Gina was cold so I offered my jacket to her with Devin doing the same for Delila. The girls were giggling uncontrollably. This seemed to go on for a solid 30 seconds. Finally, Devin asked, "Say, man, what is so doggone funny? Do I have a something in my nose?" The collective squeal from the girls only got louder at this point and then it went eerily quiet.

Delila's diminutive eye roll made an appearance and as it did, she snapped, "Only you would think something like *that* Devin Palmer!" Then the girls took off running through the grass still giggling, daring us to chase after them. Once we caught them something truly unforgettable happened. Gina spun around and I started to say something to her. Before I could, though, she put her finger over my mouth. "Shhh, don't ruin this," she told me. This girl had a way of confusing me. "Ruin wh--..." She cut me off again, "No words Gabe, no words." Then she leaned in and put her mouth on my cheek and slowly moved to kiss my lips. Over the next 15 seconds I wasn't sure if I was dreaming or not. Strange enough, before now I never fantasized about kissing Gina but now that it was happening, I didn't want to forget that feeling.

At about the same time Devin kneeled and after kissing

PLIGHT OF THE FORTUNATE

Delila's hand got a kiss as well. Delila, ever present in the moment told him, "Boy, I have been dreaming about that kiss for almost three years...whew, you *did that*." Devin, himself, couldn't help but laugh and I wasn't going to miss a moment to bust his chops so, through my own smirk I said, "My sister knows what she wants. Welcome to your future, Dev, welcome to your future."

Truth be told, if the future was going to be full of moments like that, I was ready and willing to sign up! We all headed back to our house as our parents used the night to play cards and watch a movie while they waited for us to return. When we made it to the porch, I could hear mom, loud as ever, say, "Andrew they're back! They're back. Meet me out front on the porch." Delila dropped her head and said flatly, "Well I guess we weren't going to be able to sneak in." Gina's eyes turned sharply to her bestie, "Girl, now you know you weren't going to be able to hold water anyway," to which we all burst out laughing.

Devin's dad cracked first, saying, "Alright already, did you all have a great time or WHAT???" I spoke up first, saying, "It was cool, Mr. Palmer, we had a lot of fun." What Gina said next had us all tripping as she responded, "Mr. P, it was dope! That is the most fun I have *ever* had, even better than playing ball!" Gina's dad quipped, "Well dang, Gabriel, you showed our princess a good time, then, huh?" Leave it to Delila. She was over the moon as she said, "Man, look here, these boys were perfect gentlemen. I was proud to be on Devin's arm!" She had something more specific on her mind as she continued, "It's been real cool filling you in and all but where is the peach cobbler and ice cream at? Daddy, stop holding out on me now!" Mr. Richardson said, "I guess there is nothing left to do but get the scoop." Our mom didn't miss a beat with her response saying, "The only thing worse than Delila's competitive streak is her attitude when she's hungry!" With that said, it was time to have dessert!

As we were about to finish Mrs. Palmer asked if she could put on a little music. "What did you have in mind?" mom asked. "C'mon Sophie, there is only one kind of real music, Mrs. P said. Speaking about Earth, Wind, and Fire all the adults sounded off in beautifully orchestrated unison: *Nobody but the ELEMENTS, baby!!!*" As Devin shook his head, his response was classic in and of itself, as he stated, "It's time to start that Soul Train line!" When it came to Earth, Wind, and Fire it didn't take much to get my parents excited. Dad hurriedly took mom's hand and said, "Sophie, you know we can't let these kids show us up now." Mom couldn't contain her smile as she said, "Lead the way then, Baby, lead the way!!!"

As the night carried on it was clear that we teenagers were not the only ones having a great time. Looking into each of our parents faces it was hard to tell who was more excited, the kids or the parents watching their kids. Wouldn't matter though. Watching them watching us told us all we needed to know. When something is understood, not much has to be said. My dad always told me that you never let a woman walk alone, especially at night. When it was time for everyone to leave, he didn't need to remind me of that sentiment. Gina's parents left a few minutes before we did to allow me to escort Gina home.

As we stood on the porch of my house Delila said, "Gina, I had a blast girl, we will talk tomorrow, y'all go ahead, Devin is calling me right now." Seeing D's face Gina simply said, "Alright, girl tomorrow for sure, sleep well." Gina took my hand as I led her down the steps, "Gabe, thank you doesn't do tonight justice. I have never felt more beautiful than I do right now. I really appreciate you!" I took a deep breath before I told her, "This may be the first breath that I have taken in the last few hours because when I saw you in that dress looking so pretty, you took my breath away."

Gina was crying now. I hate seeing anybody cry but somehow, in this moment it felt right. Why? Because I could tell that what I said meant a great deal to her. As a bit of confirmation, she told me as much. I'm glad she felt that because I really did mean exactly what I said. When we got to her door, she gave me a tight hug. I wanted to hold her forever just like that. We said goodnight and she watched me go back home. Once I was back on my porch, she went inside.

I told my parents goodnight, and I went upstairs. Delila was still on the phone with Devin, telling him how great a time she herself had. She was blushing. As self-assured as my sister always seems to be, in that moment it was great to see her be a girly girl.

"Goodnight Twin," I told her as I went across the hall to my room. As she hung up with Dev, she said, "Hey Gabriel, I would be extremely interested to see you capture this night with your pen on your page because I, for once, am speechless. "We will have to see because I know that feeling, Sis, I know that feeling." Delila had one more question so, she continued, "Gabriel were we dreaming?" The only thing I could say in response was, "No, not at all! To be honest, I think the reality of this night far surpassed even our wildest dreams." As we closed our doors to go to sleep, I know the smile I had on my face was matched by Delila. We really were walking on air.

Thinking about what Delila said, I wasn't sure what I would write. But I did know what I felt. In times like this, I let my feelings become the ink, as my soul becomes the writing pad. Certain things, when written on the heart, speak entirely on their own. In this moment, I was learning a lot about myself. Certain things you hear about, others you must experience for yourself. Gina was teaching me what it meant to be admired. Out of respect for who she was to me, I was figuring out what it meant to return a mutual courtesy.

Life is a trip. After the Homecoming experience, I knew who I wanted to have accompany me on my journey. There was still a lot I was going to have to learn to begin the process of understanding. Ralph Waldo Emerson had it right when he said, "Life is a succession of lessons that must be lived to be understood." After spending this night with those I cared about most, I was truly glad to be alive.

Three

New Dimensions

I was restless. I know what Gina told me about what she felt but I couldn't help but wonder if going to Homecoming together would change the dynamics of our vibe. My dad told me that the reason that he and mom work so well together is because they were friends before they became anything else. Thinking about the situation like that, Gina and I and Devin and Delila would be off to a good start because of the friendships we had and were continuing to build. I was thinking about asking Gina to be my girlfriend, but I didn't know if I should. If she didn't feel the same way, the fact that I asked the question in the first place could ruin everything. Once again, I turned to D to see what she thought but before I could, she was knocking on my door asking about Devin.

"Big head, you sleep?" Delila was asking as she opened the door. "What else would I be doing at 3:30 am?" I cracked. "Sorry Bro I can't sleep, I have all these thoughts running through my mind about Devin," she went on to say. Knowing the feeling for Gina was mutual, I concurred, telling her, "It's the same for me." Delila's eyes shifted, "Do you think Devin will ask me to be his girl? I really would like that if he did, but I don't want to get ahead of myself." By now I was in deep thought, managing to say, "I was thinking the same thing about Gina. I mean I never saw her as more than my home girl a couple of weeks ago but man, did that change."

Knowing how important this was to my sister I offered, "If it helps, I will ask Dev what's up." Sis couldn't contain herself,

"Thanks Gabe. I can talk to Gina too and see how she is feeling about you." Right then, both of us smiled and Delila gave me a hug before she went back to her room. Once she did, I began to feel a little bit better. I was looking forward to the next day, but I was nervous at the same time. Either way it went after we each talked to our friends, things were about to change.

The next day the sound of Delila's phone ringing woke both of us. It was Gina. I heard Delila say, "Sure girl come on over, I want to talk to you anyway. I'm up." Being that it was 7:45 am I went ahead and got myself ready and shot Dev a text to see if I could swing by his crib for a minute. Once I got his return text, I headed downstairs. As I opened the door, I saw Gina on the sidewalk. She motioned for me to come over.

As I met her on the walk, she greeted me with "Good morning Babe, I mean, Gabe." She was blushing. I returned her greeting with a smile, saying, "Good morning beautiful. I don't mean to cut this short, but I'm headed to Dev's, Delila is waiting for you." "Oh okay," Gina said. "What time are you coming back?" she asked. "I shouldn't be too long. I'll text you when I am on my way back," I told her. "Alright, cool. I can't wait to see you later," she said as she headed inside.

As I made it to Dev's he was already outside. "Yo, Gabe, good morning my dude, how's it going?" he asked. "It's all good, Bro, how are you?" I asked in return. "Hey, my mom just brewed some fresh iced tea, want some?" Dev asked as he offered me a glass. I told him, "You know I'm always down for a glass of your mom's tea." Curious about my text from earlier Dev asked, "So what's up man? Your text sounded kind of urgent." Trying to be careful with my words I said, "Well, it is, and it isn't. How do you feel about the dance last night?"

He thought for a second, "Gabe I really enjoyed spending time with Delila in an environment like that. We were always cool from a distance but after spending time with her up close, I really appreciated getting to know her more formally, you know other than being at church or in the neighborhood." He continued, "I hope she feels the same way because I would hate to be the only one thinking what I'm thinking." Wanting to ease his mind I told him, "Dev, you are definitely not the only one who feels that way.

Delila is hoping the exact same thing that you are. Trust me on that."

As if Devin wasn't serious before, he was doubling down now, saying, "I don't want to overstep, and I certainly don't want to be disrespectful. Gabe would you have a problem with me asking your sister to be my girl?" I knew this was coming but even still I thought for a second before I gave my answer, telling him, "Naw Bro I'm cool with it. I would've had a bigger issue if you didn't want to ask her because that is all that she is talking about." Dev let out a long sigh, saying, "Okay, cool, I lost some real sleep thinking about this."

Staying on subject, Dev asked, "Now that I am off the hot seat, what about Gina, how are you feeling about her?" I almost cut him off when I answered, "Before a couple of weeks ago I didn't see us together but now I can't see us being apart." I wanted to know if Gina said anything to Dev, so I asked, "Did she happen to say anything to you?" He was shaking his head, "No, she didn't but when she is around you now, you can see in a good way that it's different. Did you ask Delila if Gina said anything?" As I rested my hand on my chin, I said, "Delila and Gina should be having the exact same conversation that we are having right now."

We both started laughing and I wondered to myself how long the two of us might be sitting there while we were waiting for the girls to finish their conversation. I was glad to know that Devin felt the way he did about Delila because if that hadn't been the case that news would've crushed her. Devin didn't want to waste any more time. He wanted to ask her out today. I didn't see a problem with it. I was hoping that I would be able to ask Gina the same thing. But I couldn't get ahead of myself, so until I was able to hear from my sister, Dev and I had no other choice but to wait.

By now an hour had passed and we were still sitting on Devin's porch chopping it up and trying to figure out what to do with the rest of the morning. Devin had a bit of revenge on his mind. So, he issued a challenge, telling me, "You and Gina owe us a rematch. You know Delila and I had you beat!" I couldn't help but laugh as I responded, "Well why did someone who had us beat still lose?" Devin was beside himself as he said, "C'mon man nobody blocks my jumper!" Laughing still, I said, "Oh, so you have changed my name to *Nobody* now. I see how it is! I thought we were better than that, Dev!"

"Hold on Gabe, Delila is calling me, "Devin said checking his phone. "Hello, what's up lady, how are you?" he said, blushing. "He's right here hold on a second," Dev said as he passed me the phone. I was anxious as I answered, saying, "Talk to me Twin, what did you find out?" Delila didn't waste any time with her answer, as she said, "Gina would love it if you asked her out, she asked me if I had a problem with it and I told her that I was all for it." The sound that I managed to make surprised me in response. With my voice cracking, I responded, "Funny you should say that because Devin asked if I had a problem with him asking you out." "For real? Yes! Wait, Gabriel, don't play with me," Delila said, becoming overexcited.

"Sis, I'm not playing with you, he was dead serious, and I let Dev know that I was cool with it," I told her, my voice ever stern. "Well not to keep you in suspense, Twin, Gina can't wait to see you, she really is appreciative of the way you have always looked out for and treated her," Delila went on to tell me. "When are you and my man coming back to the house?" she asked me, impatiently. I motioned for Dev to come on, as I told my sister, "We are on the way right now." As soon as I handed Devin his phone back, we took off running toward my house to meet the girls.

When we made it onto my street, we could see that the girls were waiting for us. Once we saw that, we slowed down to walk, being that we were four houses down. Somehow, seeing Gina and my sister's faces sent a measure of calm over me as we made it into the yard. The girls ran to embrace us. Delila had jumped into Devin's arms, letting out a huge scream and then saying to him, "Boy this little bit of time without you felt like forever, I'm just saying." As I looked at Gina, I could only get out, "Yeah, exactly what she said," and her and I just started laughing.

Dev and I had talked about how were going to approach things once we saw the girls, so we knew we had a solid plan it was just a matter of executing it. As we fellas gazed into the beautiful faces of the ladies, I led off with a matter-of-fact statement, saying, "Girls we had a great time last night and haven't been able to get either of you off our minds." Devin continued, "A lot of things in life don't make any sense, but when we are around you two, everything does." Then standing across for our counterparts, Devin and asked the girls in unison, "Would you do me the honor of being my girlfriend?" In response, both girls, in unison as well said, "Yes!"

Gina had tears in her eyes as she took my hand, saying, "Gabe this really means a lot to me, to know that you think so highly of me, I want to experience so many great things with you and I hope this strengthens our friendship and doesn't take away from it." I kissed her on her cheek and then told her, "Gina, it is my honor to call you my girlfriend knowing you were and are my friend first."

Devin told Delila, "I lost some sleep wondering about this, but I am so glad that I'm not dreaming because looking into your eyes is so much better in person." Delila was blushing now as she said, "I've been dreaming about you for three years, but the reality of the last two weeks has more than made up for it." As my sister leaned into kiss Devin I was wondering if she was going to let him up to breathe. Gina was thinking the same thing because she said, "Dang girl, let the boy up for air!"

The mood then turned playfully serious as Delila changed the subject, asking, "So Gina when are you and Bighead going to give us our rematch?" Not missing a beat, Gina said, "I already know I don't need approval from my man for this one because there ain't nothing but air, opportunity, a ball, and a hoop in the back, Gabe, let's show these two clowns what's up!" I didn't even have to respond because Devin had already gone to open the gate to the back yard. "Delila let's go ahead and get this payback," Devin told his girl. Delila was already putting on her headband and tying her hair back, when she said, "No doubt, let's get it!" Gina returned my glance knowingly, as she said, "Gabe they don't have a chance, you know what it is!"

This rematch was intense, not that any of us expected anything less. It was back in forth for a solid twenty minutes with neither team letting the other get anything more than a two point lead up to that point. One would think that the guys would guard the guys and the girls would guard the girls, but our girls have not

TRE LaVIN

one ounce of back down in them. They were setting just as hard of screens as we were and fouling just as hard. It was clear that there would be no cheap baskets in this game. Delila through Dev a lob and I caught a knee to the jaw that knocked me a bit woozy. He made the basket to tie it up, but it was now Gina and I's ball.

"Babe, I'm a little dizzy, I'm going to clear out and set the screen so you can get a clean shot. I'm going to have to decoy." Her eyes were locked in on mine as she said, "I got you, Boo, let's set it up." Gina lined up to take the ball out and Delila checked up. "Hold up, Gabe, you alright Bro, I didn't mean to catch you like that," Devin said, apologizing. "All good man, that's what they make ice for, let's finish the point," I told him, still clutching my jaw.

As Gina got the ball back from Delila I inched up to set the screen, but Devin didn't bite. So, I came to the top of the key to receive the pass from Gina. On the catch Devin was right on my hip so I spun away but Gina had to hold the ball because my sister wouldn't give her any room. That was one thing about Delila. As good as she was on offense, she prided herself on playing tough defense. It was her calling card, and she took getting scored on by *anybody* personally. But I know if I could get Gina a clean look the game would be over.

I waved to Gina and signaled for her to run the same action again, hoping that this time she would be able to shake free from my sister. As I came up to set the screen this time Dev bit on Gina's fake trying to slide over and trap her with a double team. As he moved to trap her, he ran full speed into the pick I used to set the screen on Delila to free up Gina. Because they both got caught in the action of the screen, Gina had all the room she needed to release her shot. I didn't even have to look at the hoop when Gina said, "Off glass and game." I knew the shot was good. As frustrated as Devin was watching that shot go in, when Gina made it, all he could do was tip his cap.

"Devin did you and my brother eat yet? I'm hungry," Delila said more as a matter-of-fact than an actual question. "No not yet but I sure could eat right now, are we good to stay?" Devin asked in response. Before Delila or I could answer my mom motioned for us to come inside, saying, "Gina your mom and Devin's dad called to say that you both could stay over and have lunch with us, as they both have some errands to run." Gina was excited by the offer and shouted, "That's what's up Mrs. Clarkson, I'm down." Looking over at Devin, Gina said, "Come on man you heard the lady, and you don't want to see your girlfriend's attitude when she's hungry."

Gina's statement caught mom by surprise, as she asked, "Girlfriend? Wait, Delila what did I miss?" Looking mom straight in the eye, Delila said, "You heard that right mom, Devin asked me this morning and I accepted!" "Well, congratulations you two," mom said before Gina cut her off. "Actually Mrs. C., Delila is not the only girlfriend in the bunch, Gabriel asked me this morning as well, and I too, accepted," Gina said excitedly. Mom was practically beaming now, "Andrew is going to be so excited to hear this!" Mom went on to reaffirm something to all of us, saying, "You kids have done alright for yourselves, just make sure you continue looking out for each other like you always have and everything will be fine, you hear?" Not missing a beat, we all responded, "Yes, ma'am!"

Mom had put some ribs, chicken, corn, and potatoes on the grill, so the entire house had that good smell permeating through it. Somehow, having barbeque in this spot just felt right. Devin had his eye on a particular piece of chicken, so he made sure to ask, "Mrs. C. where is Mr. C. at? Will he be joining us?" Mom, knowing exactly what Dev was up to, told him, "Devin he will be joining us, but you can have that chicken breast over there in the corner, I came prepared!" Before we all finished making our plates my dad came downstairs and noticing everyone with their wide smiles, said, "Good morning all, aren't we just a happy bunch this morning? It's going to be a great day!"

By now you know Delila couldn't wait. As she ran to give dad a hug she said, "It already is a great day daddy, you'll never guess why?" "Why is that?" dad asked? Brimming with excitement Delila said, "Devin asked me to be his girlfriend and I accepted! This day just keeps getting better." As he grabbed a plate, dad turned to Devin, saying, "Alright son, if you treat my baby with respect always and value who she is, you and I won't have any problems. Is that understood?" Extending his hand and looking my dad straight in the eye, Devin answered, "I would have it no other way, sir, your daughter is worth that and more." As Devin went to sit back down, mom called Gina over, asking her, "Sweetheart do you have something special you would like to share?"

Gina was almost surprised to be put on the spot, but she took it in stride. As she composed herself, she said, "Yes ma'am, I do. Mr. Clarkson I am honored to now be your son's girlfriend, effective today," unable to hide her excitement either. "Good for you," my dad would say and as he turned his attention to me, he said, "Son, the exact same thing I said to Devin applies to you but understand if you ever mistreat Mr. Richardson's daughter you will have to deal with him and me!" Knowing I had two great examples of how to treat a lady, I told my dad as much.

After lunch Devin and I decided to challenge our ladies to a game of spades. By now, I could see Gina beginning to get comfortable in this new skin she was in. She was ever confident when she said, "Gabe I never want to see you lose but when it comes to spades, if you aren't on my team, there is no way in good conscience that I can let you win. No offense, Hon!" Knowing she was dead serious, as I looked down at my cards I said, "Absolutely none taken!" As we all sat around the table looking at one another Gina said, "Guys, just know I am excited for the future ahead for the four of us. I can't wait to continue making memories that will last for a lifetime." Dev put his cards down and motioned for Delila to come over to him. Once she stood by his side and handed him his glass of lemonade, he said, "I would like to propose a toast to my girl, her brother, and his girl, to the best friends a guy could have. May we be unafraid to embrace where these new dimensions are going to take us." We all held up our glasses and shouted, "CHEERS!"

Later that afternoon my heart was full. My parents were happy for me and my sister. Devin was happy. Gina was happy. The four of us were laying a good foundation for what was to come. I had been on the phone with Gina for three hours before I realized that my phone battery was about to die. We said goodbye, knowing we would see each other a little later. As I hung up the phone and put my headphones on my head, I took out my pen and found my writing pad. Once I settled in, I wrote this:

PLIGHT OF THE FORTUNATE

The Feels

My heart is a uniquely open book
On which I write an amazing hook
My thoughts scribed across lines
That become frozen beautifully in time
Those lines become the script to a score
That highlight a brightly lit future full of more
To look into your eyes is to become mesmerized
Full of allure those baby browns keep me hypnotized
In that moment I can't wipe the sudden mist from my eyes
As truly, for the first time in my entire life, I know what it feels to be alive

Four

The Seed of Disruption

Everyone has that one friend or relative that allows you to do things with them at their house that you would never be able to do at your own. For me, Devin is that friend. See, as much as my parents love a great game of cards, dominoes, and the like they despise playing for money. The one time that dad even had the slightest thought of gambling, something that happened altered his thought process and still shapes the narrative for him today. Sometimes one parent can tell a story and leave out certain details which leaves the other to have to fill in the blanks. But when it came to telling this story that was not the case. Mom can fill in every single detail. The conviction that they both tell it with makes me cringe every time I hear it.

Let dad tell it, this specific event changed the entire course of his life. When he was a sophomore in high school he was balling at the park on the Saturday after Christmas. It was a normal day. Nothing out of the ordinary was going on. I've heard this story often enough that I can tell it in my sleep. The usual crowd had gathered to watch the teenagers play a two-on-two basketball tournament. The weather was unseasonably warm, so the organizers decided to hold the event outside. As the tournament made it down to the final four teams a few of the old heads started a loud commotion at the far end of one of the courts. Apparently, someone was on a bit of a hot streak and was not shy about letting everyone hear about it.

"Come on with it," one of the men could be heard saying.

TRE LaVIN

"No way man, I ain't going until this clown shows me his hands. How do I know the deck ain't loaded?" One of the other men was trying to play peacemaker. With his arms outstretched and a steady sense of calm in his voice, he said, "Look now, keep it down. This isn't about us. We came to watch the tournament and see the young kids' ball; NOT act like kids." Dude wasn't trying to hear that though. He was convinced that the deck was loaded. "Alright, alright, I'll watch the game, but this is far from over," the man could be heard screaming in full throat. Things were still hostile, so the tournament organizer pulled out the bullhorn and said, "C'mon now, settle down, we are now ready for the semi-finals." After a couple of minutes, things had calmed down enough to get the game started.

Dad and his friend Courtney were on the court absolutely taking the other team to the woodshed. When dad gets to this point in the story his throat always tightens and his gaze narrows. Then, without fail, he hesitates before he continues, and then he makes sure to sit down if he hasn't already. Having heard the story so many times I understand why. At this point, dad tells of a noise that he hasn't been able to shake for twenty plus years. A woman came across the far end of the court in a hurry, shouting at her husband, "Jerry, put that down, don't do that! He doesn't deserve that! JERRY, JERRY!!!" The scream that rang out next sent chills down the spine, as dad recounts.

There was a thundering rattle, something resembling scattered firecrackers. It was sharp and sudden, almost like a backfire. The sound itself was unmistakable and deafening. The bleachers quaked as everyone ducked and ran for cover. Multiple shots rang out, with two clanging off the flagpole. Dad isn't sure exactly what happened next, but he locked eyes with the gunman, who was laser focused on the gentleman who raised all the fuss during the card game before the semis started. The gunman's deep voice reigned down as he approached his target.

"GIVE ME MY MONEY, FOOL, THIS IS YOUR LAST CHANCE!!! YOU'VE KEPT ME WAITING FOR THE LAST TIME!!! HAND IT OVER!!!," he shouted, reloading the gun. The man from the card game looked to be in his mid-forties, with graying sideburns and deep wrinkles in his brow. It looked like time had been more enemy than friend to him. He looked like he didn't take the gunman serious even as the gun was being cocked again. "$550 belongs to me and there will be no IOU's either, Sucka!!! Your pretty lady can't save you now. It's time to collect," the gunman said, eerily calm at this point.

A high shriek came next as a woman could be heard screaming, "NOOOOOOOOO!" The sound of her scream shook the gunman and made him flinch. People were still running and trying to take cover. By now, the gunman had another target in his sights, a fifteen-year-old girl. Dad is always sweating by this point in the story. The girl was cowering with fear. As the gunman took aim on his new target dad scrambled to get to her. The weapon jammed. Dad took the girl to the ground. "You don't own me, and you are going to have to kill me because I ain't got nothing for you," Mr. Card Game could be heard barking as he reached into his jacket.

With the gun now cocked again, multiple shots rattled through the air, followed by the sound of shattered glass. Mr. Card Game slumped over in a pool of blood, still holding his shattered bottle of Crown Royal in his hand, having been hit twice in the stomach. The gunman got away as everyone was still scattering. 30 seconds of pure terror was followed by complete, shaken silence. Most times by this point in the story mom is holding dad and rocking him. As his voice cracks, I remember dad saying, "$550! That man died over $550! It didn't have to go down like that."

Before this Saturday in December dad had never seen the girl he took to the ground to protect. That look he saw in her eyes in that moment caused his instincts to take over. Everything happened so fast, and the girl looked completely helpless, having been frozen with fear. As he stood her up there were no words and there didn't have to be. Looking across the court, seeing Mr. Card Game laying dead with his severed bottle, they both ran full speed for the next 6 blocks trying to get away, not entirely sure where they were headed. When dad said that this moment changed his life forever Delila and I were sure it was because of how close he came to dying that day. "Yes and no," he was always sure to tell us. "In that moment," dad would say smiling, "seeing how close the end was, I saw a new beginning because the girl that I ended up saving that day would later become your mother."

This is where mom likes to take over, saying, "Whenever things get tough for your dad and I, we think back to that moment and we know that we can endure and overcome. Knowing that he was willing to shield me from a bullet, I know how deep his love for me truly runs." She always tears up here, with a deep sigh, and goes on to say, "People talk about what they would do if this happened or that happened, but being with your father in that moment, I actually **know**. I know it and I fall deeper in love with this man because of it." Even as I remember that story now, I can see them just as clearly as if they were standing right next to me and telling it again themselves.

As I said before, Devin is that friend who I can do things with at his house that I wouldn't dream of doing at my own and Gina's house represents the same for Delila. One night while I was at Dev's, I was giving him the business in Madden and after beating him for the fourth time in a row, he was visibly frustrated. "Dang, Gabe, I won't keep losing like this the rest of the night, you are ringing me out," he was saying. He might have been laughing but he was hotter than a firecracker. He wanted to hit reset after turning the ball over for the third straight possession there was no way I was going to allow that, as I told him, "I don't need your charity but since you are in such a giving mood, don't stop now while I'm on a roll."

Devin redirected his focus to something else and as he did, asked, "Hey fam, what do you know about dice?" I had no clue where he was going with this, so I was shrugging when I told him, "Not much but enough to know that I don't really want to know much either." Devin doubled down, saying, "Just like when you taught me to play bones, I want to teach you to shoot craps. This way we will have something else to do and I can still find a way to hold on to my pride." Before I knew it, I had burst out laughing, telling Dev, "Alright man, if it will help you save face."

As the last game of Madden ended Gina was calling me. I was happy to see her number pop up on my phone. I made John Legend's "All of Me" my ringtone for her. When Dev heard that song, he knew he needed to call my sister, and reasoned, "I know if I don't call my girl, I risk getting buried twice in the same night.

PLIGHT OF THE FORTUNATE

I can't go out like that. While you are talking to Gina, I'm going to call Delila." Knowing how my sister gets when she doesn't hear from Devin, I cracked, "Yeah, man do that, right now, yesterday because I'm not trying to hear about this when I get back home." As I answered my phone Gina was laughing. "Hey Love, what's up sweetheart?" I asked. A sense of relief accompanied her laughter as she answered, "I just needed to hear your voice, because this homework wore me out."

"You must be talking about that history assignment," I told her. "Exactly right," she said, yawning. She continued, "I wish I didn't have to volunteer earlier because I would've have been able to study with you and finish long before now." I knew the frustration she was experiencing. Trying to console her a bit I said, "At least it's over now. Are you going to my house or is my sister coming to you?" Just then, there was a knock at Gina's window. As she put me on hold, she said, "That's her right now Gabe." Everyone had the same idea for real because Delila couldn't get her phone out of her pocket fast enough to answer Devin's call.

"Hey Twin, don't be beating my man too bad, I'm too tired to be lifting all of his self esteem right now," I could hear Delila say as she came into Gina's room. My sister knew how ruthless I was playing Madden and once she realized what she said, she deadpanned, "Girl, never mind, poor Devin never stood a chance. I have my work cut out for me now." I heard Devin come back into the room and as he did, he told my sister, "I don't need you to prop me up right now Baby, I'm about to teach your brother a thing or two about shooting craps." The confidence that Devin had lost in the last two hours playing video games had slowly crept its way back.

Delila turned serious, telling Devin, "Don't you go burying my brother now, I know how you get when you start plotting revenge." Dev was snickering now, "C'mon now, Delila I have to be able to win at something, you three have been whupping me too long. Let me make it." After about ten more minutes on the phone Dev and I said goodnight to the girls.

It was time to learn how to play dice or "shoot craps" as Dev would tell me. To make it easier for me, he passed me a sheet of paper with the following rules:

TRE LaVIN

> When rolling, only use one hand
> Always keep the dice in the sight of other players
> Make sure both dice hit the wall, or the roll won't count
> 7 and 11 on the 1st roll is an instant win (pass)
> 2, 3, 11, or 12 on the first roll is an instant loss (craps)

I was already confused but I was intrigued. Devin said he would break this all down in greater detail, but he wanted me to know the basics of the game first. "Okay by me," I told him. Over the next few minutes, he would go on to explain the different ways to bet and such but he knew I wasn't going to play for money. He and Gina had heard my parents' story about that fateful day when they were sophomores in high school and he knew it wasn't going down like that but because he was good at the game and his dad taught him, he wanted to teach me. We spent the next three hours playing and by the time we went to sleep, I had a decent understanding of how to play but it would take some time before I would be any good.

I didn't know it right then, but Devin was planting small seeds of disruption by teaching me to play this game. Once I learned to play, I knew that I would eventually have to master it. I was too competitive to have it any other way. When Devin and I played there was no money on the line but whenever it came to learning anything competitive it wasn't worth playing if we couldn't keep score.

Devin was hell bent on making sure he would have a leg up on all of us somewhere so when the girls came over to his house the next day to kick it with us, he made sure to teach them the basics too. Confident in his assertion he would tell all of us, "Craps is a great game to play, made even better when you learn all the ins and outs. For all the luck it takes, you have to think the game too and I have one heck of a mind!"

Delila couldn't believe her ears, "Boy are you listening to yourself? You take vanity to a different level entirely!" Gina was hysterical as she said, "Devin, I knew you didn't like losing, but I didn't know you took Gabe beating you so many times at everything else, *this* hard!" As my sister and I joined in the laughter, all Dev could do was shake his head.

PLIGHT OF THE FORTUNATE

    Gina was still feeling some type of way about the history assignment that we struggled with and said, "I need some real assistance. Please help me get ready for this exam on Monday." Delila, ever confident in her abilities, was almost borderline cocky when she said, "Look best friend, the three of us are going to make sure you won't be struggling with this thing come Monday morning. Tell us what we need to do." The thing about the four of us was that at any given time either of us could be the smartest person in the room. We were great at cultivating each other's strengths that way and encouraging each other.

    I had an idea, and I ran it by the group. "Maybe if we put all of this stuff to music it will be easier to make sense of it for you Gina. What do you think?" I went on to ask. Thinking on it for a second, Gina said, "Ok, Gabe, what did you have in mind?" I had Dev give me a beat and I started putting the pertinent happenings of our American history in the 1920's and 30's to the beat. Delila put a little melody to it and before you knew it, we had come up with a song that not only gave Gina confidence but also helped the rest of us as well. After committing the song to memory, we couldn't wait to test it out in class on Monday.

    History class was 1st period for all of us so we would find out quickly if my idea worked. Being that we everyone finished the exam in the first half of class we got our grades back before the end of the period. I got a 94, Delila got a 92, and Devin got a 90 but we knew that we would score high. Gina was a nervous wreck as she took the exam as evidenced by the constant shifting that she kept doing in her seat and the way she kept twisting her hair around her finger as she twirled her pen. So, we were all waiting to see what she scored.

    Being that she turned her test in last she was the last one to receive her grade. When she got her test back, she couldn't look so she asked if I would. I turned over the paper and proceeded to lift her up off the ground. As I did, I kissed her cheek and told her, "Gina, you aced it! Straight 100%. I'm proud of you." The fist pump that followed almost took me out, but I was happy for her, nonetheless. Because we had success with this study method, we decided to utilize song creation as a memory tool with any of our major tests going forward.

TRE LaVIN

There was something tranquil about Gina and her presence in that moment. Her eyes sparkled with a glimmer that perfectly accented the height of her chocolate complected cheekbones. Her natural curls had been pulled into two perfectly coiffed afro puffs and the cherry lip gloss she wore made her lips glisten as she spoke to my sister while walking into the hall at the sound of the bell. Knowing how she made me feel then I made myself a promise that said, "If there was anything she ever needed and I could provide it, it was hers." There was nothing better than seeing her excited and I wanted to make sure that I always did my part to make that happen.

At lunch that day, Devin broke the dice out and as he did, he said to me, "Alright kinfolk let's see what you've learned." This request caught me by surprise, and I asked, "Right here? You want to do this now?" "Yeah, why not?" he answered equally surprised by my question. My tone turned serious, "I don't know how I feel about doing this at school, man." That infamous Devin Palmer smirk surfaced as he said, "Dang, man it's not like we are playing for money! Relax!"

Devin was resolute and stubborn to say the least. He was even trying to set a certain mood, deciding to play DMX's "Party Up" as he shook the dice in his hand. As the music started, Dev began bobbing his head, saying, "Gabe, the good dice players have a certain rhythm to the way they throw. Hold the dice too long and risk throwing everything off." This dude was so serious, it was almost comical. "You serious, man?" I asked him. Devin didn't even look my direction. He just kept bobbing and as he did, he said, "You have to a get a rhythm to the rock, like this." By now my best friend was holding court and all eyes were on him. He was soaking up all this attention. Somehow being able to teach others about something he was good at was exhilarating to him.

Delila was liking the confidence that her man was showing in this moment. Not wanting to leave her out, Devin said, "Delila come sit next to me beautiful." Delila was beaming as she said, "Do your thing Devin, baby, I love watching you work!" Over the next five minutes as everyone saw how hot Dev was, the smile on his face just kept getting bigger. As many questions as I had when Devin broached this idea, by now, there was no denying

PLIGHT OF THE FORTUNATE

that he had found his niche. Devin Palmer was intelligent and tackling the books was never going to be a problem for him. In this moment, however, I learned that he was not going to be caught not having a hustle to get by on either. Thinking about my friend's innate ability to grind also led me to think how thin the tightrope he could walk was. Cue that loose-leaf:

Trouble
Playing a game of chance can leave one mining for fool's gold
As even the shakiest confidence finds the courage to be bold
Lessons to be learned seem to find abstract ways to be taught
Because things deposited can become both empty and lost
The true cost of self-sacrifice and its circumstances never fully considered
Until you're walking through a mine field of
shrapnel left from casings of bad decisions
The blowback from the explosion leaves nothing
but scattered dreams never realized
And a puddle of blood and tears from the skies left over from a lifetime
Of failing to reach for the help of others who
offered the security of a lifeline

Five

16

Sweet sixteen was coming for my crew and we were excited to throw a big blowout. Devin's birthday is two days before mine and my sister's, with Gina's birthday one day after ours. So, there was going to be a huge get together at Gina's to celebrate. I had been saving my money for a while to get Gina a charm necklace that I knew she liked. When we had gone to the 16th Street Mall that was all she was talking about. I knew that I couldn't go wrong getting her this gift. Devin, on the other hand, was going to get Delila a rare edition signed copy of a script from Porgy and Bess one of her favorite musicals. His mom knew someone that worked at the Tattered Cover bookstore and her point of contact had just gotten the copy of the script in.

"Devin, let me take you and Gabe over to the Tattered Cover, the script came in," Mrs. Palmer told him as we came downstairs. "Alright mom, let me get my wallet," Dev responded as he ran back up to his room. We left to go get the script. When Dev saw it, he did a little shuffle and let out an "Oh, Wow!" The script, we found out, was an original copy that had been signed by the cast and was in mint condition. This copy would have gone for about $1,500 but Devin's mom was a friend of the family and they owed her a favor, so he only had to pay $200.

"Mom, thank you so much, Delila is going to love this! I can't wait to see her face when she gets this," Devin said as he got the bag off the counter. Knowing how happy Devin was, I told him, "Dev, I can really see how much you love my sister. This is something that she won't soon forget." "She is more than worth it, Bro! I am more than honored to do it," he went on to tell me. Once we finished up at the bookstore Mrs. Palmer took us to the mall so I could get Gina's necklace.

My dad had placed the order for the necklace for me because I wanted to have it engraved. The inscription was to say: *G & G, 4ever 2 B!* Upon my dad's suggestion I placed one of our Homecoming pictures inside the locket itself. I remember looking at this necklace when I first saw it but seeing it now with the personal touches blew me away. Now that we had the girls' gifts secured, we headed back to Dev's crib.

Right around the same time, Mr. Richardson took Gina and my sister to pick up the gifts for me and Devin. Mr. Richardson helped Gina get some signed Denver Nuggets memorabilia and some floor seats for all of us at the home finale against the Sacramento Kings. Delila managed to get the same type of stuff for Devin from the Colorado Rockies as well as tickets to the Rockies home season opening series behind home plate against the Chicago Cubs. It helped that all of us loved sports because we always had a great time whenever we all got together to either watch or attend games. For all intents and purposes things were coming together nicely. The only thing left to was to have the party.

Delila and I's birthday is April 12th but to accommodate everyone the party was to be held on Friday, April 10th, which was Devin's actual birthday. When the day came there was all kinds of excitement. From what my sister told me, Devin and I were going to enjoy our gifts and I informed her of the same regarding her and Gina. Delila also told me that there was a very sweet gesture that she and Gina were extending that Devin and I would be sure to appreciate. In fact, it was that very gesture that the girls wanted to extend ahead of the party, so they asked us to meet them in the park.

When we got to the park the girls handed each of us a letter. Delila told us that they each wanted to put into writing how being with us for the last year and a half made them feel. Devin opened his first. It read:

PLIGHT OF THE FORTUNATE

Dear Devin,

First, I want to wish you a very happy birthday! I hope that it is everything that you wish for it to be. Being your girlfriend for the last 19 months has been an amazing experience for me. You really understand me, and I am truly grateful for that. As I told you in the beginning, I had been dreaming of being your girl for a long time before it actually came to pass. I am so glad that my crush turned into the beautiful relationship that we both now share.

Watching my parents and yours, I see what a beautiful future is supposed to look like, and I hope that we can have a relationship like the ones that are modeled in our households. I love how you are not afraid to hustle and grind for what you want. Your no quit attitude is something that attracts me to you more and more each day. I also like how you support and encourage me to be my very best in everything that I do. It really helps to know how much you believe in me!

I want you to know that I don't just love you, but I appreciate you too. I really look forward to what is coming next for us and can't wait to continue making beautiful memories with you.

Loving you before you even knew, today, and beyond,

Delila

For some reason, watching the expression on Dev's face as he read his letter got me really anticipating what Gina had written to me. As I got ready to open my letter, Gina was blushing. Mine read:

Dear Gabriel,

Happy birthday, Sweetheart! You and Delila have been my best friends for as long as I could remember! But just over a year and a half ago my life truly changed for the better. I see that you have taken wonderful notes, paying expert attention to how your dad treats your mom. You are a real gentleman and I am honored to be your girl! I really enjoy spending time with you, and I love it when you look deep into my eyes.

TRE LaVIN

Why? Because you were the first person other than my parents to see something deeper in me. You saw a beauty in me that I didn't even see in myself! You showed me that to be pretty was not just a way to look, but more importantly, a way to feel! I feel different around you. I feel special! The way you make me feel makes me want to see you achieve all your dreams. Also, I can't wait to see what dreams we can achieve together!

You really mean a lot to me and I just wanted to take a little bit of time to tell you that. When we are together, I know that anything is possible. I can't wait to see what happens as I walk out this beautiful future with you!

Love Always,

Gina

Man, I knew that Gina loved me, but for her to express it the way that she did made me feel valuable and important. It was one thing to have my parents tell me how much they loved me or to have Delila tell it but Gina letting me know her true feelings was next level. Being that this party was on a Friday night, we wanted to make sure we were back at Gina's before 5:30 pm because Mr. Richardson let us know that there was a special presentation that the parents wanted to make to us and that portion of the program was supposed to start at 6:15 pm after all the guests had arrived. There were about 30 of our friends showing up and with Spring Break due to officially start the following Monday getting people to come was not an issue because most people were leaving on Saturday morning if they were headed out of town.

When we got back to the house, there were beautiful floral arrangements waiting for us. Mr. Palmer was a horticulturalist who worked at the Denver Botanic Gardens. Because of his contacts there, he didn't have a problem getting a favor called in for the occasion. Getting the entertainment to flow just was a specialty of Mrs. Palmer, a live event planner, who worked down at the Ogden Theatre (The Ogden, as known by the locals). With her personal touches added, she didn't disappoint!

Mrs. Palmer also had the food catered for us. She got food

PLIGHT OF THE FORTUNATE

from Delila's favorite soul food spot, located in the Five Points neighborhood, called Welton Street Café. On the menu tonight was oxtail stew, jerk chicken, yams, fried cabbage, red beans and rice, potato salad, sweet potato pie, and rum cake. My mom was going to cook but the Palmer's insisted she get a night off to truly enjoy the festivities. Once she heard where the food would be coming from, she was all in as Welton Street Café is one of her favorite restaurants too.

Leaving the park, we all decided to head home quickly, freshen up for the party, and meet back up at Gina's at 5:30 pm. The girls each had sun dresses that they were going to wear, and Dev and I had jeans and smooth button downs that we were going to wear, untucked. Devin made sure to put on his favorite cologne, Fahrenheit, and I put on mine, Cool Water. Delila put on Light Blue by Dolce and Gabbana and Gina went with White Tea by Elizabeth Arden. Devin and I had already been to the barber shop and Mrs. Richardson had done the girls' hair, so we all were confident in how we were going to look for the evening.

Everyone gathered in the Richardson back yard to start. Dad got the music going and set the vibe. Once everyone showed up, we were all asked to come into the living room and gather around. True to form, Mr. Richardson started his presentation at 6:15 pm sharp! "We parents are so very proud of the four of you and, at the risk of embarrassing you, we just wanted to show how much we love you," he said, chocking back tears.

The slide show started with pictures of each of us and the day we were born. Then pictures reflecting different milestones in our lives were shown: first crawls, first steps, first tooth in, first tooth out, christening, first day of school, first sports, memories, and the like were all put on display. Sure, we were all a little bit embarrassed, but you only turn sixteen once, so we didn't mind too much. Mrs. Palmer followed with an original song that she wrote and had the girls' crying. Then Mr. Palmer and Mrs. Richardson set up the dart board and set all of us up in teams for a little impromptu dart tournament, which turned out to be a lot of fun, especially for Dev, because he finally beat all of us at something the first time through (never mind he had a lot of help from my sister)!

Next up though, my parents told all of us to come outside. Once we were all out in the front yard, they directed our attention down the street and told us to watch. "What are we watching for, Mrs. Clarkson?" Gina said excitedly. "You'll see, Sweetheart, just hold tight, my mother told her, waving her arms toward the left of where we were all gathered. Suddenly, all these headlights began shining at once. The bright lights had all of us squinting through the bright glare. "What's happening, Daddy?" Delila was saying, sounding completely confused. "Hold on baby girl, you are about to see, just wait a few seconds more," my dad told her, knowing that he could not keep his daughter in suspense much longer.

Still not knowing what was going on, we watched four 2013 Nissan Altima sedans pass. When they didn't stop, we all were really confused. Then, the cars came back around and stopped at different intervals. Once parked, someone got out of each car and came to Devin, Delila, Gina, and me with envelopes and car keys. In unison, all four people who got out of the cars said, "Happy Birthday, these are gifts from each of your parents." All I heard next was Gina's squeal, only to be outdone by my sister's high pitched scream.

We each received a car from our parents. Mine was black, Dev's was silver, Gina's was metallic gray, and Delila's was brown. I was completely blown away, "Dad, are you serious, right now?" I said, not able to hold my excitement. "Yes, Son, very much so. You all earned and deserve it! Happy Birthday!" My mom could be heard next, shouting, "Well, everybody get in and check them out!!! Go ahead, it's okay!" Now that we all knew what was happening, we didn't waste any more time. Between the horns blaring and the lights flashing the party had officially begun!

We all got in the cars and took them around the block. I couldn't believe that we just got cars for our birthday. The party itself was already amazing but to get these cars was astonishing! After our lap around the block we all parked the cars and headed back inside. Once back in the house, the entire lower level was turned into Club Clarkson. Jazz, hip-hop, R&B, pop, and gospel were all on the playlist. For the next two hours we had a blast with our friends and family as we celebrated this once in a lifetime occasion together.

PLIGHT OF THE FORTUNATE

    This party was just the beginning of a truly amazing weekend. The next day we would head to Coors Field for a 6:10 pm first pitch to watch the Rockies play the Cubs. We were extra excited being that the Rockies had started the season 4-0. In the short time that the Rockies had existed, dating back to 1995, this was only the second time that they had won the first four games to start the season. The Rockies would end up losing the game 9-5 but it didn't stop us all from having a great time. There was a Rooftop Live! Concert with Andy Rok and The Real Deal. This was cool to be a part of because Andy "Rok" Guerrero is a Denver native whose group Flobots we were all hug fans of, especially their songs "Handlebars" and "Rise."

    The seats behind home plate were nice and so was the atmosphere. We were able to get a Justin Morneau bobblehead because we were part of the first 10,000 fans to gain entrance into the stadium. We also got to meet the Rockies manager, Walt Weiss, who was the shortstop for the team in their early years of existence. For all of us to be there with our families was truly special. There is just something electric about the LoDo (Lower Downtown) District of the city when the Rockies are playing. Blake Street is full of energy and life.

    As if that wasn't enough, we would all head to Pepsi Center the next day to see the Nuggets play the Kings. We had seats directly behind the Nuggets bench. George Karl, who coached the Nuggets for nine seasons, made his return to Denver as coach of the Kings. It was fun to see him back being that the team had so much success under his watch. We were disappointed that we didn't get to see DeMarcus Cousins or Rudy Gay, two of the Kings best players play. But they were injured so we understood.

    Kenneth Faried, the Nuggets young forward, had himself a ballgame, scoring 30 points. Wilson Chandler chipped in with 9 rebounds, and Ty Lawson had 11 assists. All the starters scored in double figures. The Nuggets started fast in both the 1st and 3rd quarters and were able to beat the Kings 122-111. The season itself was a struggle for the Nuggets as they only won their 30th game of the year against 50 losses but you wouldn't have been able to tell on this day.

    Pepsi Center holds 19,520 people at full capacity and this

game only had 14,000 in attendance but it was still a great day to take in a basketball game. The experience itself was made all the better because of who we had with us. After the game we went over to Larimer Square and had dinner at Russell's Smoke House. I had to get the smoked chicken wings, baked beans, and cast-iron cornbread. Gina got the ribs and coleslaw. Dev had the pulled pork and mac and cheese. My twin had the fried chicken and potatoes. All our parents were in a burger type of mood. Overall, the food was an experience for the entire palette.

At some point throughout the night, I found a way to get completely lost in Gina's eyes. I also stole gazes of all our parents and Devin and Delila too. Words didn't need to be spoken. There wouldn't have been enough money in the world to separate me from the purity of that moment. What I was looking at was priceless! I had a front row seat to the beauty and ascending depth and levels of love at its finest.

This was one of the times that the adults made sure to show us a fine example of what an investment in each other was supposed to look like! I didn't have to look at television or a movie trying to fantasize about what true love looked like. Our families really took time to ensure that this weekend was not going to be one that any of us would ever forget. If I could've bottled this weekend up forever, trust me, I would've. We all would've. It was a high point for us all.

16

To turn sixteen was sweet
Made even better by my sweetheart
And the gestures of family
With memories worthy of Hallmark
Images taken in through sculpted lenses
Of a camera whose film was lovingly developed
By the effervescence found in the five senses
Awakened through anticipation of what's to come

Six

Impactful Decisions

After turning 16 our sophomore and junior years of high school seemed to fly by. Denver East High School, home of the Angels did so much to nurture our growth. There were Sadie Hawkins Day dances, Valentine's Day dances, and even the Winter Formal. Throw in football games in the Autumn, basketball games in Winter, and baseball and softball in Spring and there was always something to do. But there were separate events that shaped the narratives of what each of our futures were going to look like and each happened during junior year.

For Devin it was running for Student Council President. Devin's popularity was never in question and he did right to capitalize on that. But he found his niche when he led a sit in to protest the suspension of a student who was punished for refusing to cut his dreadlocks. He couldn't understand why a student's appearance had even become an issue especially because the kid had been inducted into the National Honor Society and was a straight A student who didn't fit any other stereotype except that he had the audacity to be born Black and chose to accentuate the strength of his heritage by growing out his hair. After these events transpired, Dev really thought he might have a future as a politician.

Gina had an opportunity to be a teacher's aide and found out how much she liked putting projects and things together in classroom environments, especially being able to tutor and mentor students who were struggling in history class. Learning about people on a deeper level really interested her. She used her semester as an aide to really cultivate these interests and add many valuable tools to her toolbox, thereby sharpening her mental aptitude. beyond that, she really gravitated to African American History and found a unique and impactful connection to it. Her ability to absorb and process information was on full display during this time.

Delila refined her beautiful soprano voice on the stage as she got to play Bess in Gershwin's *Porgy and Bess*. Her rendition of "I Loves You, Porgy" had everyone in the auditorium hanging on every note. The full spectrum of her vast talent was on display in this production. Her singing was phenomenal, but she garnered the greatest praise for the acting chops she exhibited. She really took everything in this performance to another level. They say the best actors and actresses play parts so well that they become the characters in the process of the production. Delila truly made everyone a believer as they watched her. I always knew that my sister was talented but after watching her on stage in this production I was sure that she was going to have a wonderful future on any stage she wanted.

I became the editor-in-chief for the school newspaper, *The Spotlight*. I was able to really find and shape my voice with various creative writing submissions. Doing research on current news stories and being able to bring life to things that had a direct impact on the student body helped me learn the basics of what it was going to take to be not only effective as a journalist but how to write things that were full of substance and left the reader with something to ponder and move conversations forward. It was rewarding for me to get feedback from my peers and begin to see the power of print media. I knew that I wanted to do something that would bring a voice to those who couldn't speak up for themselves.

The great thing about what was happening was that I got to see passion and growth in my crew. Watching Delila, Devin, and Gina in their element brought me a great sense of joy and allowed me to connect with the deeper purpose within myself. One of the highlights of the year was when I got to put pieces into the paper that got to spotlight the great things that we were all doing in the same issue just after Delila wrapped production on the school play. To have all our names in print at the same time was an amazing feeling of worth and accomplishment.

Delila and I signed up to do some volunteer work at the Boys and Girls Club to not only give back but to earn community service credits for college. We both knew that doing so would look good on a college application, but it was deeper than that for us. We each had been attending the Boys and Girls Club since we were six years old and had grown to have many positive memories there. Now to be able to help the kids coming behind us begin to write their own history was something that we both took great pride in.

The four of us spent a lot of time volunteering at the local food bank as well. It was a great way to keep us all humble in my dad's estimation. I got a big head once and started to smell myself a little bit. That didn't last long though. My mom put a stop to that immediately. She doesn't yell much but in one instance I put her on the other side of mad. I had complained openly about the food bank not having a name brand version of a product and mom wasn't having any of that.

As she was staring a hole through me, she said, "Gabriel Clarkson, how do you know that you won't ever end up here needing the very services that you are complaining about? Today could be name brand central but tomorrow you could be a member of no-frills nation." Just when I thought she was done, she continued, "You're one medical emergency or short paycheck from finding out firsthand. Favor isn't fair and lack doesn't discriminate!"

It was my close-minded arrogance that drew the ire of my mom, and dad certainly wasn't going to stand for that either. He tightened the screws even more when he said, "Son you live good because your mother and I allow you and your sister to do so. You haven't even begun to understand what it truly takes to earn a living!" Knowing it was too late to escape his glare, all I could do was drop my head as he sternly reminded me, "I can take every privilege you think you have. Your mother and I have rights, the only right you and your sister have at this stage is the obligation to act accordingly. Do you understand?" After that, there was nothing else I could do but answer, "Yes sir," and pull my head out of my fourth point of contact.

After seeing how my parents laid into me, the others knew not to complain, even about the slightest perceived inconvenience. As my dad reminded me, "For us, not having something is a mere inconvenience, for others the inconvenience of not having basic necessities was a bitter way of life." After this, he never had to ask me which side of that fence I wanted to be on. My parents were big on making sure that we were put into a position to understand the plight of others. They really wanted to ensure that we were going to be an effective part of solutions, not reasons to exacerbate a problem, especially if it had already reached a systemic level.

It was at times like this that my parents did a great job of getting our attention so that we would know not to bring unnecessary attention to ourselves. Mom was the one to make sure to drive this point home, saying, "Gabriel and Delila, no matter how good you think you have it, you can never forget the skin you're in and the unspoken burden that comes with it." With tears in her eyes she said, "You never want to be someone's point to prove or quota to make. That will NEVER end well!"

With all the things we were beginning to see on television around this time in the news, and in recent memory, her point was well taken. By now we were still less than five years removed from any number of crimes committed against young Black males. Tamir Rice, 12, was shot on a playground in Cleveland, Ohio after having the toy gun he was playing with mistaken for a real one. He was shot almost immediately after officers arrived on the scene.

Michael Brown, 18, was killed in Ferguson, Missouri after an altercation with police, shot six times, after being followed for having stolen a box of cigars from a local convenience store. Be that as it were, Brown was found to be unarmed at the time of his death. What followed in the city of Ferguson was pure and utter chaos and civil unrest that lasted days.

There was no way to shake what happened to 17-year-old Trayvon Martin, who was killed in Florida while walking back from the store after buying candy and something to drink. A local man who had been on the neighborhood watch took matters into his own hands after believing that Martin looked suspicious and after an altercation shot him dead. All these cases were both frightening and disheartening especially given the fact that all three victims were between the ages of 12 and 18 at the time of their deaths. Recollections of these instances made my mom's words penetrate on a much deeper level. None of our parents wanted to be the next one to bury a child.

    Mr. and Mrs. Palmer always made sure that Devin was doing something to challenge his mind. They never wanted him to have to depend on the stereotypical things that got others ahead in life. They wanted him to have a mind worthy of distinction and one that allowed him to effectively challenge the process of the status quo. Because of this, when having conversations with Dev's parents, there was never one truly correct answer. We were always challenged to think beyond the walls that others had put up. We were encouraged to not only find ways around those obstacles, but especially to knock them down, while building a foundation for new standards and ways of thinking in the process. If an answer came too easy, the Palmers always encouraged us to investigate to figure out what was missing and begin to look for the hidden truths in what people were not telling us.

    Mr. and Mrs. Richardson have always been deeply in touch with their history and made sure to pass the importance of this down to their daughter. When Gina and I started dating, Mrs. Palmer told us, "As the two of you embark on this journey never forget who you are, where you are, and where you are trying to go. As you begin to walk down this road, you have one distinct advantage…each other." There was great value in what she told us that day and I have never forgotten that. The foundation of this sentiment goes a long way toward explaining why Gina gravitated to African American history the way that she did. The deeper beauty in this was the fact that Gina was not okay simply being a part of history, she wanted to make her own, letting people know at the end of the day that she was here for a purpose, *on purpose*.

    Knowing how invested our parents all were in our collective wellbeing we wanted to do something in the next seasons of our lives that was going to matter. We were encouraged to network and build contacts not only at school but especially in the community. My dad taught all of us to find one commonality with every person that we meet. At one point he told all of us, "If you look close enough you may be surprised to find out that we as a society are more alike than we are different." Trying to make sure that we didn't miss the point, he continued, "The only thing that separates us from solid understanding is fear of what we have either never known or of what others have been afraid to teach us."

As we would come to find out, people are often intimidated by what they don't understand and are afraid that if someone has access to the same tools that have allowed others to succeed, those same people may get left behind. This is especially true in the Black community. As a people we have spent so much time oppressed that we often are unable to recognize the seeds and fruits of progress. Our people have spent so much time having to defend themselves and fight that they have been ill-prepared to ascend when it was time to take flight. As sad as that was to know, it was a truth that we had to own and pay attention to because we were not going to be able to outrun the harshness of that reality any time soon.

We all wanted to have the opportunity to make our own choices and not be placed into a vacuum where those choices were made for us. My mom taught all four of us about the power of belonging in any room or meeting that we walked into. She often said, "When you walk into a situation, people may underestimate you but how you respond to that is not up to them, it's up to you." In one instance, Gina was struggling with this concept and my mom knew it, so she took some extra time with her to guide her into a deeper level of understanding. My mom would go on to tell Gina, "Sweetheart, they may underestimate you going in but make sure that they have to account for you, your viewpoint, and your value coming out. You are a commodity, NEVER a liability!"

We were all taught to gain and cultivate skills that were always going to be in play. This was important because none of our parents wanted to ever see us set up to get played. Mrs. Palmer told Delila once, "Listen, the table is where all the action happens, but one will never know that if they don't first get a seat and once you get that seat excuse yourself when you are ready never have them force you away." The point was that representation matters and it is made that much more valuable when representation is armed with wit and intelligence that can disarm short sided viewpoints and ignorance.

With these things in mind, pressure was building. It was time to apply to colleges. The four of us all had the grades necessary to get into any school that we wanted to. There were no assumptions to make but it was the first time since we were 14-year-old freshmen that we had to look at the possibility of being somewhere else separate from one another for an extended period. Did we want to go to school in the city? What about the state? Or did we want to go somewhere else entirely?

First there were the individual decisions to consider. What would we major in? Would the schools we were interested in have those majors or would we have to think about a different path to take? What career field did we want to consider? What about scholarships? If we decided to go to different colleges could the relationships that had grown so strong ultimately survive? Before we could even explore answers to those questions, we had to take the SAT's and ACT's first.

The four of us had been studying and felt good about where we were being that we had done well on the PSAT test a few months earlier. But that was a *practice* test. We didn't want to be overconfident to the point of being arrogant, but we didn't want to overthink things either. The SAT itself was supposed to take about 3 hours and 15 minutes but we also knew that the essay portion could add another 50 minutes to the day as well. On test day we were told that we could expect to be testing from around 8:30 am until 1:00 pm in the worst-case scenario. The ACT, on the other hand, was to take roughly 3 hours to take, which would become 3 and a half hours with breaks.

With our senior year of high school now upon us we decided as a collective to take the ACT in September and the SAT in October to give us enough time to take the tests again if we needed to better our original scores. We knew that within about ten days of our scores coming back, colleges and universities would start to get our scores as well, so we wanted to give ourselves the best opportunity to maximize potential official visits and such.

Nothing about this process was fun. The pressure was felt by all of us. Of course, we felt it from our parents. That wasn't their fault. They just wanted us to do our best and be able to live with the results. The problem was that we were all putting extra pressure on ourselves when we didn't need to be doing so. We had put the work in, and the evidence had shown itself, we just had to trust that the proof was in the pudding and the results would manifest themselves in the outcome that we all desired.

We all had G.P.A.'s north of 3.6 so the academic side of the coin was not a concern for any of the four of us. Before we could even begin to explore what we might study we had to take those aptitude tests to see how we stacked up not only against our peers but also against the different admissions requirements for the schools that we were considering wanting to attend. Lucky for us, we were going to be able to take these test a mere three weeks apart.

On each of the test days we all did what we could to lend support to one another, but we knew that ultimately it would come down to us as individuals once it became go time. Looking back on it now, we each severely over thought the exams themselves and were a little too high strung going in but that had nothing on the heightened level of anxiety we would all feel as we awaited the test results. One Friday afternoon during school we were informed that we should expect our scores in the mail by the time we got home. We decided to meet over at Devin's house to find out the results together.

Being that we were at Dev's house, he opened his scores up first: 615 in reading, 617 in math, for a total of 1231. Gina went next: 624 in reading, 633 in math, for a total of 1257. Delila then opened hers: 610 in reading, 603 in math, for a total of 1212. As I held my envelope in my hands I was overcome with sweaty palms and nervousness. What if I didn't do as well as the rest of the crew? Finally, I ripped open the envelope: 636 in reading, 640 in math for a total of 1276. There was a huge collective sigh of relief once all the scores were revealed because we knew that our scores and grades were good enough to meet the minimum requirements to attend any school in the state of Colorado and even beyond, if that is what any of us would choose to do so.

The same scenario played out almost exactly three weeks later on a Thursday. For the ACT score reveal we decided to meet up at Gina's after school. Once again, the host's house dictated the order, so Gina went first. She got a 28. Next was Devin. He managed a 26. I didn't want to wait to go last this time, so I left that honor for my sister. In the meantime, I scored a 30, with Delila chalking up a 27. As another collective sigh of relief went out, we then began to figure out what each of us wanted to major in.

Drawing on the impactful experiences that we each had as high school juniors the year prior made this process a little less nerve racking. I knew I wanted to pursue a degree in journalism. Period. End of story. Delila was trying to pick between something in music, theatre, or a combination of the two. Devin really had done a lot of research on what politicians and lawmakers do since the sit in at school, so he just had to narrow his scope slightly. Gina, though, seemed to be having the most trouble, trying to decide between studying social work or African American studies. All of this would be predicated on which schools we were able to get accepted to.

The girls went outside for a few minutes to get some air and get a better understanding of what they wanted to do. This choice was not one that was going to be taken lightly and they were both jealous of the fact that Devin and I were already certain about what we wanted to study. After about twenty minutes outside the girls came back with their verdicts. Delila decided to study theatre and Gina decided on ethnic studies, knowing that some of her core classes for either of the disciplines she wanted to pursue would transfer if she made the choice to change her mind.

The next choice was where to apply. We had some great choices to pick from too. We could stay right in the heart of the city and go to the University of Denver. We could go 15 miles west of Denver to the city of Golden and attend the Colorado School of Mines. There was also Colorado State University in Fort Collins, just over an hour from the city, and the University of Colorado at Boulder, which was a 40-minute drive from home. Each of these colleges had a lot to offer us as prospective students while also giving us the opportunity to remain close to home. Over the last handful of weeks, we were all sure of one thing: we wanted to go to school in state. That decision also took a different type of pressure off each of us regarding our romantic relationships because the worst-case scenario would have us no further than an hour away from our significant other(s).

Ultimately, the decision was made for the four of us to apply to those four schools as well as the University of Northern Colorado, which is in Greeley, once again, roughly an hour from Denver. As much as we were there to support one another we were all hoping that we would each get into all the schools so we could make a final decision about where to spend the next handful of years of our lives.

Over the next two weeks we would all have deep discussions about all the scenarios that were going to be in play depending on what decision the colleges we applied to would make. Devin and I had separate conversations with the girls as well as a conversation with each other. The same was true for Gina and Delila on the other side of the spectrum. If we were not going to school with our significant other(s), how often would we see them? Would we spend fall, winter, and spring breaks at school, at home, or on someone else's campus altogether? What would happen if Delila and I didn't end up going to school together? Lastly, we considered what it would be like for all of us to attend the same college. Exactly ten days after we all applied to the different collegiate institutions, we were told to check both our email and our mailboxes as a decision would come through both platforms.

Decision day would come quickly and this time our entire families were on hand to share in the moment with all of us. Our parents got home before all of us, so they found a unique way to deliver the news to each of us. This time we were all back at Casa de Clarkson for the presentation. Another slideshow was set up with each of the college logos prominently displayed. Then each of our faces was shown over the top of each logo if we got in. To the delight of everyone involved we each got into all the colleges we applied to. The greater reveal would come a few minutes later

PLIGHT OF THE FORTUNATE

as each of us was going to share our decision on where to attend school.

To add to the drama of the situation, none of us had shared our decision with anyone before then. Not our parents. Not our siblings. Not our best friends. Not our significant others. So, we were all on pins and needles trying to see what the future was going to have in store for each of us and our relationships to boot. Delila took the bull by the horns first to reveal her decision.

"First, I want to say thank you to all of you for all of your continued support. I wouldn't be here without you. It means so much to be able to make this announcement in the presence of the people that I love," she began. Choking back tears, she continued, "With that said, I will be majoring in theatre arts and furthering my education at the University of Denver," she said excitedly. Devin held his breath, knowing that he was still to reveal his choice. But he would have to wait until I revealed mine.

"As my Twin said, thanks are for all of you because I don't make it here without you. I appreciate the legacy that my parents have built, and I am excited to hear that Delila will be furthering that going forward," I said resolutely. Looking directly at my dad I took a deep breath and said, "Saying that, I feel that I need to spread my wings and fly away from here. I will be going forward wearing the black and gold, majoring in journalism, as I attend the University of Colorado at Boulder next fall."

Devin was next. He got straight to the point, as he said, "Exactly what the other two said. Delila, it's me and you together at DU baby. I am Pioneer bound to study political science. I really appreciate the strong legacy that is being built on that campus, and I want to make my mark there also."

Now, that just left Gina. Devin and Delila would be attending school together but would Gina and I get to do the same? I was hoping so, but I would have to understand if she made a different choice. I did want her to have the best. Yet, in the moment I was feeling vulnerable, knowing that all my best moments had been with her and I didn't want to imagine any time where that wouldn't be the case. But here we were.

Gina, then broke out the following, "I could've gone any place but ultimately I look best in black and gold, so Flatirons (shoutout to the iconic rock formations that call Boulder home), here I come, where I will major in ethnic studies. I want to be able to take what I am passionate about and really make a difference. You have given me a purpose and I can't wait to fulfill it. Thank you all. Gabe, it's me and you against the world, Babe!"

In the end there was nothing to worry about. I was happy. My sister was happy. The people we loved were happy. More than that we could all see how proud we had made our parents. It really felt like this was a moment that we were all invested in. Devin and Delila were going to be 45 minutes away from Gina and me but we were still going to be close enough to share in special moments going forward. With our college decisions out of the way, it was now time to finish strong and make our senior year of high school one we would remember from here to eternity.

Seven

Profiles in Courage

A person never knows the depth of their strength until they are completely broken amid true weakness. The worst part of what was coming was that treating someone with the utmost respect, a respect that was eventually shown to be undeserved, didn't hold any weight. None. The gravity of the situation was about to test the very fabric of who we all were. When really taken to task, we were all about to find out that love was much more than a four-letter word.

My mom sent me to the store to pick up a few things for dinner. As I was pulling into the parking lot there was a huge commotion. Some people were arguing across the parking lot. As I was getting out of my car, I called Gina to see if she was going to stop by for dinner. She said that she would but not until after she finished her homework assignment. Because what was going on had nothing to do with me, I continued to mind my business and do what I was sent to do.

I hadn't been in the store for ten minutes and it was not going to take me ten minutes to get back home. When I got a few blocks from home, I passed Dev and Delila as they were walking to the park. They didn't need a ride so I continued home knowing that it would not be too long before I would see them back at the house.

As I approached an intersection, the light was changing from yellow to red, so I came to a stop. Once the light turned green, I began to pull away, only to be pulled over by a police officer. I knew I wasn't speeding so when the sirens started blaring, I was genuinely surprised. However, I was calm because my parents taught us exactly what to do if we were ever pulled over by the cops. Once I stopped, I immediately pulled out my license and registration, placed my hands on the dashboard, and waited for the officer to approach.

A White officer approached from the rear of my vehicle and ordered me to produce my license and registration. I spoke in an even tone, asking, "Good afternoon officer, can I ask what I failed to do?" The officer sounded hurried and impatient as he said, "We have reason to believe that you were involved in an altercation at the King Soopers on Colorado Boulevard about 20 minutes ago." As I looked directly into the officer's eyes, I said, "I did leave from there not too long ago, but the commotion had already started when I arrived. I got what I needed and started my return home. I didn't stop to see what was going on. It didn't concern me, sir."

The officer was shocked for some reason. "Are you sure that was all you were doing over there?" he asked me in an accusatory tone. "Yes sir. With all that commotion going on, I just wanted to get home." I guess my answer was not good enough for him because he was yelling now, "Get your behind out of the car, NOW!" I've had enough conversations with my parents to know not to say anything, except to answer questions directly as they are asked and to cooperate fully so not to make the situation worse.

"Yes sir. I am removing my seatbelt so that I can follow your instructions," I told him as I was trying to do exactly what he asked. "Look Boy, are you deaf? I know you heard me! Get a move on, NOW! I don't have all day," he said, still yelling. By now, a couple of people had pulled up and taken out their cell phones and started recording. "Put the phones away, there is nothing to see here," the officer could be heard telling the bystanders.

"Hurry up Boy. Get the lead out of your butt and move," he told me, fully incensed. The next moment brought swift change as the situation escalated. My driver's side door was flung open, and I was jerked out of my seat and thrown down to the concrete below. "You couldn't mind your own business, huh? You just had to make it a point to disturb others who were simply going about their day," the officer shouted as he removed his handcuffs. Things were happening quickly. I could hear everything the officer was shouting at me, but I was honestly confused because I knew I hadn't done anything wrong.

"Don't you move! Stay still! Do what I say, you will be sorry if you don't! You WILL NOT get away with this!" the officer said as he continued his rough handling of me. "What did he do wrong?" a woman who was nearby could be heard asking. "Mind your business, ma'am, this situation doesn't concern you," he snapped back. Right about this time, Mr. Palmer was riding past. He immediately called my dad who had just made it home.

"Say Drew, you and Sophie need to get down here right now. A police officer has Gabriel pulled over and is rough handling him on the ground. There is a crowd gathered. Get here quick," Mr. P. said. Mrs. Richardson and Gina had just made it home also when my parents came rushing out of the house. My mom called Delila to find out where she and Devin were. "Stay where you are, we are coming to get you, the police have your brother pulled over and it's not looking too good. Don't move! Your dad and I are coming right now," she told my sister as dad pulled out of the driveway.

Within two minutes my parents, Mr. Palmer, Mrs. Richardson, Gina, Devin, and Delila had all shown up on the scene. As my mom got out of the car, she could be heard talking to one of the women. "Excuse me, ma'am, can you tell me what is going on here, that is my son over there. Did he do something wrong?" she was asking. "No ma'am not at all. Apparently, there was an altercation down at the supermarket on Colorado Boulevard and they think your son had a part in some altercation," the woman told my mother.

One of the other men who had witnessed the events recognized my father immediately. "Hey, AC, I got the entire thing recorded on my phone, Gabe didn't do nothing wrong. He has been nothing but cooperative, but this cop has one hell of an ax to grind," he told my father. The precinct got word of the situation and how quickly it escalated because just after my parents arrived, three other police cruisers pulled up and started barricading off a section of the street.

As this was going on, I was being lifted off the ground. The sound of my face being bounced off the hood of my car was unmistakable. One of the other officers seeing what his colleague had done, rushed the officer who had stopped me and took him to the ground. "C'mon Davis, that wasn't necessary, this kid is no threat!" the officer was shouting as he got the officer who had pulled me over off me. "Turn the bodycam off man, turn it off now," Officer Davis could be heard telling another officer. "Can't do that, D, you are on your own, too many eyewitnesses," the officer told Davis in response.

Another officer could be heard saying, "They have the two assailants from the supermarket altercation in custody down at the station. They have been positively identified." By now another bit of commotion started. Someone shouted, "Well if you have them in custody, then what is all this about? Why is this young man being roughed up and profiled like this?" He got one of the officer's attention, as he said, "Look, I will write whatever statement I need to and talk to whoever I need to. I have this entire incident on camera, recorded." Two other witnesses let the officer know the exact same thing.

Someone else summed up the confusion and commotion perfectly when he said, "What was this young man's crime, driving while Black, in black? There is absolutely no way that this is ever going to fly!!!" It would be a few minutes before things would start to calm down but, in the process, dad had his lawyer hat on and was taking statements from witnesses knowing that what was coming next was going to be one heck of a nightmare to sort out. But before anything else could happen I had to be taken over to Presbyterian/St. Luke's Medical Center to be checked out.

I was visibly shaken. I was not able to fully process what had transpired. Had I really done something wrong? Did I say something to anger that police officer? I really didn't know. When someone from the police precinct met us at the hospital, they informed my mother that I "fit the profile and description" of one of the suspects who had robbed a store earlier in the day and had gotten into a fight with another man over some money in the store parking lot where I was sent to pick up the groceries.

PLIGHT OF THE FORTUNATE

My parents wanted to know what description I was supposed to fit. Some bulletin had gone out stating that a warrant was out for a light skinned Black male, 6 feet 5 inches, and 225 pounds, who drove a black 2013 Nissan Altima sedan. The only thing that was correct in that entire description was the year, make, and model of the vehicle. Delilah and I are both brown skinned, her standing 5 feet 10 inches and me standing 6 feet tall. On my best day, I am lucky to tip the scales at 175 pounds, with Delila checking in at 150 pounds herself. This enraged my parents, the Palmers, the Richardsons, and everyone who had been witness to this gross level of misconduct displayed by the officer who pulled me over.

What was his motive? Why did he go so far? What was he attempting to cover up? These were all relevant questions. My family and those who cared about me were not the only ones searching for answers. By now, word of this unfortunate happening had spread throughout our community and there were protestors lined up on the streets. The discord had reached fever pitch as I lay in a hospital bed. No one that cared about me would see the first signs of sleep any time soon because we had just received word that a press conference to discuss what had happened was gong to take place at 9:00 am the next morning at the police precinct.

Everyone was trying to get a grasp on what happened and why it even occurred in the first place. Devin was ready to fight. Delila was having a serious anxiety attack and Gina couldn't stop crying. Nothing was making sense. There were no words, no answers, and no solace to be found. Even worse, there was nothing anyone could do to even begin to pick up the shattered pieces of my innocence that were lost once my body hit that concrete, and a man took his ignorant insecurities out on me, making me his punching bag and whipping boy. Every emotion that could be felt in that moment was. The purity of the human spirit was lost once that officer tried to take mine.

Gina and my parents tried their best to get me to rest but it wasn't working. Every time I closed me eyes all I could see was that officer jerking me out of my seat onto the ground. My wrists hurt from the handcuffs. I had a serious migraine headache and my face bore the bruises and scars from my bout with the hood of my car. For all intents and purposes, it looked like I just finished a twelve-round prizefight for the light heavyweight championship of the world. In the hours that followed, my parents would work on a statement to release to the press, one that would not only provide an update on my physical condition but also let everyone know how I had been affected by the reckless negligence of the officer who was ultimately charged to serve and protect me but by all accounts, had failed.

Emotions had boiled over. Tempers were short. News coverage had begun to take on a life of its own. Everyone wanted one thing and one thing only. Answers. Not excuses. The only thing standing between the confusion we had and the clarity we needed was time. 9:00 am couldn't arrive fast enough. But before we could even approach that bridge, we had to cross the one that would see us over and through the night ahead. Being that it was only 7:00 pm at this point, we were going to need all the help we could get.

I was restless. My parents tried playing music to change the mood. Delila and Devin tried to crack jokes, but nothing was funny. Gina sat by my bed trying her best to bring me comfort. Nothing worked. Laying in that hospital bed I was angry! How could this happen? What would the police say to attempt to justify this man's behavior? When I did finally get to sleep, I was awakened by the still fresh flashback of having my skull bounced off the hood of my own car, in my own neighborhood, a few blocks from the safety of my own house. I am a forgiving soul but admittedly I was seeing red and the way everyone in the room was processing things, that was not going to change anytime soon.

Just after 8:30 am the next morning the news stations and camera crews began assembling in front of the hospital. Because of the protestors in the streets and where I was in the hospital the locale of the press conference changed. All our parents went downstairs to meet with police personnel ahead of the news conference. We kids were left upstairs in my hospital room to watch the news conference from there. The district attorney welcomed everyone who had assembled, thanking them for their time. She led with a statement that read:

PLIGHT OF THE FORTUNATE

"Good morning, thank you for coming. This is a sad day and an even more disturbing situation to have to address as a 17 year-old high school student of this community is laying upstairs in a hospital room trying to process the despicable treatment and malice that he was subjected to just yesterday afternoon."

Next, my dad was introduced and standing with my mother, read the following:

"The Clarkson Firm stand to represent Congress Park resident and Denver East High School student Gabriel Clarkson. This, however, is far from a simple case because I don't just stand here as a lawyer representing a client. My wife and I stand here as parents seeking justice for the racial profiling and discriminatory treatment of our son. We ask that you respect our family's privacy as we lend support to our son in this difficult time. Physically, Gabriel is in a great deal of pain but that pales in comparison to the emotional trauma that he has suffered and continues to endure as a result of this unexplainable act of cowardice carried out by one of our men in blue. We will not make anymore statements today but would like to thank everyone for their continued encouragement and support for Gabriel and our family. We will not rest until we have justice for our son."

What the police chief said next set off an absolute firestorm of confusion. He read the following statement:

"We do not condone the behavior exhibited by Officer Davis during the traffic stop that occurred yesterday afternoon. It is unfortunate that young Mr. Clarkson was subject to the volatility of someone, who while going through a tough time of his own, temporarily lost his head and executed poor judgment. As of this moment, Officer Davis has been placed on administrative leave indefinitely pending our investigation into this matter and all that has taken place."

TRE LaVIN

As Delila heard this, she was livid. Devin tried all he could to calm her down but that was NOT going to happen. Period. All Gina could do, once again was cry. With all the news being made regarding police misconduct I knew that what happened to me was part of a bigger problem, one that didn't have a simple answer. The good thing for me was that despite the pain I was in, I was alive at least and my parents were not being forced to bury one of their children. From my vantage point, however, the statement that was read by the police chief didn't provide any sort of proper explanation for something that made no sense to any of us and could not be explained.

As for me, I had my sister give me my phone. I was in too much pain to write but I was able to put my feelings into focus, making sure to record the following poem, which Gina would write out for me later. I was tired and my family was hurting. The community was up in arms. But as a people, we were totally exhausted. We had grown weary of watching those who were supposed to protect us try to explain why they couldn't. In this case, especially, it was completely disheartening to hear them try to justify the officer's behavior by saying that he was going through a tough time of his own. For him to do what he did to me was no temporary lapse in judgement it was a permanent excuse for ignorance, a form of disease we were no longer willing to accept. Speaking into my phone, I recited the following:

Enough

We. Are. Well. Past. Fed. Up.
Enough. Is. Enough.

Kindness is not a weakness to be taken through dis-advantages,
but cowardice is a scab that can no longer simply be bandaged
and I am exhausted; enervated of medicating your problem
the symptoms of which, at this point, are beyond incurable
because you continue to ingest the serum of not knowing
hoping that we will be oblivious and somehow continue to miss
the reprehensible behavior directed at those you willfully dismiss
but we are far from blind, we heard what you said

PLIGHT OF THE FORTUNATE

thinking we are stupid, as I now lay in this hospital bed
we see you and we now know the depth of your sin
but before you start, no I am NOT about throwing stones
just informing you that your hatred is no longer hidden
and now you must answer for what you refuse to atone
we are supposed to forgive but your actions make that tough
so, for your sake be glad we have a Savior that we can look up
and that the true vengeance of what you deserve is not up to us

We. Are. Well. Past. Fed. Up.
Enough. Is. Enough.

When I finished, complete silence fell over the room. There were no dry eyes. They say a picture is worth a thousand words. The still shot of what we felt in that moment was one that told a story of hurt and despair. A couple of the nurses on the floor had been watching the news conference and had come into my room as they heard me reciting this piece. They couldn't believe the high level of strength and character that I had exhibited in that moment. One of them even relayed that she had never seen the depth of pain so intricately wrapped.

While none of us would wish this treatment of our worst enemy, I couldn't separate the feelings I was experiencing in this space. What was once so clear was now clouded. People were no longer hiding the subtleties of racism behind glorified smokescreens. The enemy we all knew existed long before this day was now bold enough to stand in plain sight and furthermore, had the audacity to act like what had occurred was somehow okay because someone was in the midst of going through a tough time on a bad day.

The news conference was still going on downstairs but once I finished detailing what was on my heart in poetic form, mentally I checked out. My body wasn't the only thing that was tired, my soul was spent too. Within twenty minutes the news conference would end, and all our parents would join us back upstairs. Once everyone had reassembled, Delila played the clip of what I just recited. At this point I completely lost it, weeping openly, totally inconsolable.

TRE LaVIN

My parents stood on either side of my bed. Gina held one hand and Delila held the other. Mrs. Palmer began to pray. When she finished everyone in the room vowed to bottle this feeling and use it to bring justice in a way that had not been seen before. My mom concluded, "Gabriel, the world is about to find out how strong you truly are because they will have no choice but to profile the courage you are putting on display and account for the truth." My dad was visibly upset as he said, "Sophie, as true as that statement is, by no means does that make this right! I'm ready to fight and I'm not just talking about legally. Gabriel is 17! This is personal." There was no calming him down and everybody knew it. All we could do then was hug each other.

They kept me in the hospital for four days for observation. I had mental health counselors come to see about me and all of us. The news coverage continued. Everyone wanted to interview me to find out more about the person I was and how this could have even occurred. My parents were not willing to give the news people that type of access. Within the clutches of this situation I was already left unprotected. My mother, especially, was not about to allow the vultures to circle just so I could be left uncovered again.

The rest of the crew went to school, but it proved difficult because everywhere they went, they were bombarded with questions about my condition or the specifics of what transpired. Devin even went as far to say, "Bro, I would've them rather done this to me because I can't stand to see you going through this. I really care about you man and I hate that we can't take matters into our own hands and do more. I feel completely helpless." I understood what Devin felt but he was right. We couldn't try to fix this by dishing out our own form of rogue justice. That would be extremely counterproductive.

The best thing to do, according to my dad, was to exercise calculated restraint. My dad would go on to state, "Gabriel, they may have tried to beat you out of your mind but the way to win this fight is to beat them by using ours, no matter how much that would hurt in the short term." Mr. Richardson and Mr. Palmer agreed, however begrudgingly. We didn't want to simply put a band-aid on the situation, we wanted to get things pushed through that would bring about radical and lasting change!

It would be a while before the legal process would flush itself out enough to possibly bring these events to trial and a situation in which Officer Davis and the police department would have to answer for and provide a detailed account for themselves, their treatment of me, and their actions. In the meantime, life had to go on and there were still things that had to be accomplished, like finishing my senior year of high school. As difficult as it would be to turn my attention to that, I did but I also kept a very long memory, so I would never forget what injustice itself felt like.

Given all that took place I knew one thing for certain. I would not be fighting this battle alone. My family and friends were with me. I had the support of my school and my church. But more importantly, I had an entire community behind me that would not be satisfied until they had plausible answers and justice was served!

Eight

Quicksand

For a solid week after my release from the hospital I had trouble finding motivation to do anything. I was scared to leave the house, fearing that I would be forced to endure a similar fate again. Outside of my family and closest friends I didn't know who I could trust. Yet, I knew for certain those who I could NOT trust; anyone who wore that blue uniform. I know that I wrestled with bouts of insecurity before this but now I couldn't be sure of my own name.

I've heard stories of what some people endured while overcoming their own personal hell. I never imagined, at 17, that I would be staring my own battle directly in the face. One thing is true of adversity. It will make you touch parts of your psyche and soul that you never knew existed. While going through therapy, I was encouraged to journal and write out my feelings, no matter how raw. My therapist gave this bit of unique insight, saying, "Gabriel, rawness is the sibling of reality. Touching it will allow you to eventually free yourself from the makeshift prison that this incident and your subsequent emotions have placed you in."

Initially, I couldn't free my mind enough to write. Honestly, I feared what the raw reality of my emotions would bring to the surface. My parents and everyone else associated with me had been through enough and I didn't want something else that I was feeling to make things worse. They were already going through enough. I didn't want the pity of others feeling sorry for me, especially at school. But the truth was, at times, I was stuck throwing the same type of party that I didn't want for myself.

TRE LaVIN

When I was outside with Gina one afternoon, someone slammed a screen door...LOUDLY! That startled me so much that it scared Gina too. I began shaking violently. I wanted to run and hide but instead, I froze and cried. I had no clue how to process what I was feeling then. Gina sat me down on the sidewalk. Then she did the only thing she could. She held me and buried my head in her chest. Nothing was said. We just sat there, sobbing, uncontrollably.

This episode lasted for a full thirty minutes. Gina managed to call our parents and let them know what happened. Our parents then came outside and sat with us to make sure we were okay. We weren't. How could we be? This was all brand-new territory. While there was guidance for situations like this, there wasn't really a playbook because each circumstance is unique, and it isn't fair to try to attack everything with blanket solutions.

Remembering what the therapist told me, my mom offered the following advice, in the form of a question, asking, "Gabriel, honey, if I got you a pen and paper do you think you could try to write out what you are feeling? You never know, it could help. Just tell me what you need." As painful as this was, I was willing to try to do anything to feel better. With our parents there with us I knew I had the support needed to try this exercise. I just needed to find the courage to carry it out and execute. My mom brought the pen and paper and I just started writing the first thing that came to my mind. It turned into this:

Hellish
Why is it that people want the blessing of sharp, quick wit?
Until that same wit exposes other viewpoints as counterfeit
And they realize that being Black really DOES have great benefits
At least until being threatened by the mere sight of your melanin
Then, not even the best laid foundations of what it means to be intelligent
Find safe places to be displayed because stupidity
is now frighteningly common
I want to believe that there is some type of
good coming from this pain I'm in
I'm praying for a miracle I can't grasp because
this hellish reality is far from it

PLIGHT OF THE FORTUNATE

When I finished, I simply handed the paper to my dad, got up, and started to walk. My hurt melted into anger again quickly. Before I knew it, I was seeing red. I couldn't understand why this was so hard to shake. I just wanted to be okay. Honestly, though, I didn't have the first clue what that looked like anymore. In the present tense, I knew I would have to figure out a way to learn to be okay. As my dad would remind me, that alone would be vital to my ability to merely function.

When we got back to my house, we all sat down to watch television, attempting to relax. Mr. Richardson was flipping through the channels and we settled on some comedy that was on, one that none of us had seen before. We were all cracking jokes and having a good time until seeing a car crash take place in the movie sent me spiraling right back to the place in my mind that I just left.

Once again, I froze. Completely. I tried to speak but the words wouldn't come. Suddenly, nothing was funny anymore. Looking at the screen, I began to see Officer Davis's face and hear his voice. As much as I didn't want to, I was reliving my trauma all over again in real time. Rage took over. The words I was searching for just seconds before weren't so hard to find now. "COWARD! What did I ever do to you? What possessed you to think that this was okay to do?" I was yelling at the top of my lungs. Fury, until now, was an emotion that I hadn't touched. Now, it was an emotion that I wouldn't soon let go.

Gina was walking over, attempting to calm me down when her dad stopped her, saying, "No, Gina, he has to get this out. It's been a long time coming. We may never understand but we can be here. Let him have this." Gina was livid, saying, "I hate this Daddy! I feel so helpless! What will it take to make this officer feel what Gabriel is having to endure now? This is NOT okay!" Seeing the raw emotion pour out of Gina let me know just how deeply she cared about me. The feeling was mutual. I was broken. I was scared. More importantly, her reaction had me worried because I wasn't sure if she was going to be able to be all she needed to be for herself while she was trying to be everything that I needed her to be for me.

The repercussions that lingered because of this situation left all of us reeling as the holidays approached. No one, it seemed, was able to get in touch with the holiday spirit. It was like the part of the calendar that presented us with Thanksgiving, Christmas, and New Year's had taken a vacation itself. We all felt it too. The simple things that we found joy in had become chore like. There wasn't a time when everyone was okay. If it wasn't me wrestling with what happened, it was our parents, or Devin, or Gina, or Delila. Everyone was on edge. There was only one thing we knew for certain; we weren't okay. Period.

On the legal side of this equation, we hadn't heard *anything*. Officer Davis was still on administrative leave and all the police department would say was that the investigation was still ongoing. But nothing was moving and even if it was, it wasn't moving fast enough for any of us. Most days were okay because we were surrounded by people and different things that we could hide our energies in. The nights were the worst, however.

On one of those nights, one week from Thanksgiving, I was awakened by my dad, sobbing. It was 2:00 am. He had punched a hole through the bathroom wall after seeing that Officer Davis had resigned, in a statement, of all things. Though his sobs he said, "This SOB resigned this way so that he wouldn't have to face us! So, he wouldn't have to face my son! WHY GOD? You have to help me make this right, please." He was pleading at this point.

My mom heard the wall break and came rushing upstairs. I could hear her screaming, "Andrew! Babe, what's happening? Are you okay? Where are you?" Delila interjected, "He is up in our bathroom mom and he is crying. He saw something on television just now, but I don't know what." Mom, still searching for dad, told Delila, "Where is Gabriel? Check on your brother, make sure he is okay. Let me check on your dad. Andrew??? Talk to me, I'm here."

When Delila found me, I was curled up in a ball, shaking at the foot of my bed, having broke into a cold sweat. The anxiety I was feeling had gone through the roof. I asked my sister if she could try to call Gina. With the way the last month had transpired, all the families had made a pact to answer the phone, no matter the time, to provide support for one another. We all had been on the other end of that phone line for someone else too. No one was immune. Not us teens. Not our parents. None of us.

My dad had slumped to the bathroom floor, literally in a puddle of his own tears by the time my mom found him. She tried her best to console him. She knew he had reached his breaking point. He was still sobbing when he told mom, "If I could take this pain from my son Sophie, trust me, I would. He doesn't deserve this! NOT. AT. ALL." Mom knew it too. In response she said, "I know, Andrew, I know. Delila said you might have seen something on T.V. What happened?"

Dad's gaze tightened as he said, "This coward resigned from the police force through a STATEMENT! A STATEMENT, SOPHIE! What kind of BS, is that? If I ever get the chance to get my hands on him, I SWEAR, I'll..." Mom stopped him, saying, "Baby, I know you are angry. We all are. I don't know why this is happening like this but the only thing to do is trust God. Vengeance is HIS, not OURS, Drew! Gabriel is strong. Our family and support system are STRONGER! With God's help we will find our way through this." There was a long, deep pause as she continued, "I have to believe that because other that God and you, Andrew, I am struggling to believe in anything or anyone else. I love you! I am here with you and we are in this together." After another 45 minutes on the floor, my parents fell asleep right there in the bathroom, exhausted.

While my parents were trying to figure out the rage they were experiencing, Gina called me and Delila called Devin. Our significant others came over immediately to check on us. Devin had been up and saw the breaking news so when my sister called him, he already had his phone in hand to call her. As Devin pulled onto our block, he stopped by Gina's to pick her up so she wouldn't have to walk by herself.

Once inside, Delila and I met them downstairs in the den. Devin led off with, "This officer must really believe that his actions were okay somewhere in his head because it seems like this resignation was a slap on the wrist. Like this will allow him to dodge his day in court. I don't understand it at all." Gina was next, saying, "I'm sorry Gabe. I wish there were something more that could be done right now. This just seems hopeless. I'm worried that this guy will get off somehow and what happened to you will just become an afterthought. But I sincerely hope that won't be the case. What has your dad said about this?" Delila answered her question, saying, "Daddy is on the other side of angry right now. He punched a hole in our bathroom wall once the news broke. I guess they thought they could avoid a serious backlash by releasing the officer's statement about the resignation in the wee hours of the morning."

As confused as everyone was by these events I was even more so. I was beginning to question openly where I was in my life, where we all were. Just over a month ago, everything was looking so bright. All I could see were possibilities. Now, after what happened on that street, all I could see were liabilities. My vision was genuinely clouded, and the sun didn't shine the same. With all of us gathered in the den and with the news of Officer's Davis's resignation still playing on the television in the living room behind us, I wrote this:

Something Lost
I lost something and I can't seem to find
The pieces of what used to be my peace of mind
At the same time, innocence got misplaced
As memories of times much simpler got erased
Childhood told a pure and beautiful undiluted story of hope
That got swallowed by a pending adulthood spent trying to cope
Dreams set high upon a staircase whose apex I could never reach
Though that never stopped harsh realities from leaving lessons to teach
It took me a while, but I learned most of them too
Some, however, I wished for the chance to redo
Because, somehow, vivid imaginations painted on canvasses of what could be
Looked so much better than the bitterness of truths I was not ready to see

Delila dropped the water she was holding as I finished, leaving shattered glass spread across the floor. We were hoping the noise didn't wake our parents. Being how exhausted they already were, it didn't, much to our relief. Devin already knew how sick I was with a pen but even the depth of what I just wrote, shocked him. He said, "Gabriel Clarkson, I am utterly amazed

PLIGHT OF THE FORTUNATE

at the strength of your words. I am learning so much from you. Pain shouldn't have to have you as its face right now, but it does. I am honored to be your friend and brother. Justice must find a way to be done. Situations like this are what make me want to do what I want to do in college and beyond." When Devin was serious there was no changing his mind. I knew that he would do great things. Now with what happened to me, he felt like he had a purpose. The world, I was convinced, was going to be better for it.

The suspicions we all had were realized the next day as the police department, rather than face the media, released their own statement regarding the resignation of Officer Davis and worse, directed all inquires to their public relations officer. My dad, hearing this, headed straight to the office to get to work. Mr. Palmer and Mr. Richardson, knowing how mad he was, went with him to protect him from himself. In the meantime, my mom, Mrs. Palmer, and Mrs. Richardson went over to the church to pray. Things in our neighborhood were quiet over the next few days, only because Thanksgiving was on the horizon.

True to form, when Thanksgiving Day arrived, mom was in her element, doing one of the things she did best, entertaining. The food, we knew, would be amazing but the support we would receive would give us hope; a hope we hadn't had in some time. The day began with us in church, something we all needed. The pastor covered us in prayer and asked the congregation for their continued support, knowing that the hill we still had to climb would be one that would test the very fabric of our collective being.

Once we left church, our crew gathered at our house to watch the first football game of the day, a 16-13 victory for the Detroit Lions over the Minnesota Vikings. Next, we watched the Dallas Cowboys and Washington Redskins play a real good game, won by the Cowboys, 31-26. During the game we sat down to eat. Food and fellowship, in this instance, was exactly what we needed. There was music, cards, dominoes, board games, and football being tossed around the yard. We normally do this in the front yard, but I was weary of doing that, so we convened in the back yard instead.

Mom let us know that we were going to have more guests over at the house at 6:30 pm to discuss something monumental and important but she didn't tell us what that something was. Not too long after the pies and cakes hit the table, we had roughly another 30 people descend on the family home. Once everyone arrived, my parents called everyone to gather around and find a seat. Then, she asked Devin to come and make a presentation. This development surprised me because none of us knew what he was up to.

After thanking everyone for coming, Dev passed out some flyers detailing the reason we were all gathered. He took charge right away, saying, "All of you, by now, know of the horror that my friend Gabriel and his family have experienced because of one rogue officer's dreadful and despicable actions that were carried out on our neighborhood streets in October." Devin paused, and with his eyes watering, continued, "Being angry is not enough. I wanted to see if there was a deep and impactful way to begin to walk the path toward justice for my friend." He had everyone's full attention by now. Knowing this, he went on, saying, "On Monday, January 16th, which is Martin Luther King, Jr. Day, I hope to bring tangible awareness to this systemic problem in a way that will move the needle in the mightiest of ways. But to do so, we need all of your help!"

Devin wanted to organize a march that would originate from the site of my traffic stop, pass our church, and follow a route down to the Colorado State Capitol, where we would end by protesting on the front steps and demanding legislation that would hold officers accountable for the unethical treatment of not only minorities but all citizens, especially those who are wrongly profiled based on race and other discriminatory factors.

Hearing this, I began to cry. I was not expecting this, but to get this type of support on the ground level meant a lot to me. My sister came and held my hand as we both tried to process what was happening. Of course, I really appreciated Devin for what he was putting together but Delila's admiration for her boyfriend was elevated that much more, knowing what Dev was willing to put on the line for not only her family, but especially her brother.

Another reason we were assembled was so that Devin

PLIGHT OF THE FORTUNATE

could start gathering signatures for the petition he was starting. Everyone was more than willing to oblige and cooperate. Dad would take this petition with him to the law firm. Mr. Richardson would carry it with him to Thomas Jefferson High and Mrs. Richardson and my mom would carry it to the DU campus. Mr. Palmer would cover the Botanic Gardens and Mrs. Palmer would tackle The Ogden and Fillmore Auditorium to start. We also had many volunteers to circulate this petition at their places of employment and beyond.

What really made this entire endeavor special was that Devin was the catalyst for its inception. The adults in the room took extra motivation from this and were fully engaged, wanting to empower us to see the true power of one unified voice brought together for the purpose of impacting meaningful change. The night had reached a crescendo now and we were all feeding off the energy in the room.

Suddenly, the lights on our street got extremely bright, almost to the point of blinding some as they looked out the windows. Multiple car horns were sounding simultaneously, causing us to shift our attention almost immediately. Some people could be heard shouting obscenities at the same time. This commotion was followed by a ground shaking thud. "What was that?" one of the guests asked. "Not sure, but it came from this side of the street," another said, pointing toward the far side of our house.

A deep fog had overtaken our street. This seemed like it was done to distract us and divert attention away from exactly what had just taken place. Still not sure what happened, a few of the adults went into the front yard, while telling all the kids to stay back and take cover. Upon inspection, it was discovered that the thud we heard was from multiple bricks that had been thrown into our yard from the street. The two that were retrieved from directly in front of the porch had messages attached to them. One of them read:

"Keep that young man in his place or there will be more problems. Take this to trial and find out the hard way. POLICEMEN MATTER TOO!"

TRE LaVIN

I was incensed! Someone who didn't even know me or what I was about was telling me to stay in my place. I expressed myself as only I could, screaming and cussing as I did.

The Lies of the Sunlight
The fog has lifted, but before it did, my perspective shifted
From the realm of impossibilities to the jagged thorns of reality
One that if I'm being honest, I'm not quite ready to face
Especially having bricks thrown, demanding me to stay in my place
Because the vision of what I see got lost in clouds of insecurity
Damned cursed pride had me looking into the light of a sun that lied
Told me it would light my way through any storm of adversity that I'd find
And I believed it too, until the heat burned even my wildest dreams
Leaving the clarity of what I thought I was
sure of, to dissipate into that fog...

After what we witnessed as a collective, we couldn't wait for MLK Day. It couldn't get here fast enough. Christmas may have been coming up but seeing those bricks left a bad taste in all our mouths, pulling some of the grandparents in the room back to a time in our American history when our rights as African Americans were anything but civil. We were fortunate, once again, that no lives were lost in this instance. However, that did not stop some from wanting to ensure that whoever was responsible for this would get what was coming to them.

One man said, "I believe in and love the Lord with all my heart but watching and being a witness to someone or a group of individuals who is trying to take the very heartbeat of who we are by throwing sucker punches to our souls…I have to draw the line right there." We knew this wouldn't be a fair fight and mud would be slung. But now, we were painfully aware that we had to upgrade our equipment and get ready for a different type of war, the one within. The solid ground that we were standing on just minutes before had shifted, leaving us struggling to support the weight of a blatant hatred, unmasked yet again, leaving us standing in figurative quicksand.

Nine

Limping to the Finish

My senior year was becoming a high-pressure series of jagged starts and stops. Somehow, it was not terribly difficult to maintain focus on my schoolwork. I found a source of comfort in knowing that I could control that outcome when it came to my grades. After all, with schoolwork it was just me and the material. In social settings, however, I would continue to struggle mightily. My crew sensed this and started doing all they could to help me find a new normal amid all the turmoil.

First, Gina really wanted to help get me out of my funk. So, her parents got us all tickets to the Colorado Ballet's production of The Nutcracker, which is held annually at the Ellie Caulkins Opera House. This is always an amazing show! The talent of these dancers is incredible. It helped that I could get lost in the majesty of this performance. It also felt amazing to be in Gina's arms and have everyone's support. It was a challenge early on for everyone to get comfortable and enjoy themselves because they were worried about me. About ten minutes into the show, however, I was able to put their concerns to rest. It really did end up being a magical night.

Next, Mr. Palmer got us tickets to the annual Blossoms of Light extravaganza that is held every year at the Botanic Gardens. This amazing display is something that draws people in from all over to take in this beautifully expressive sight. The display of lights itself runs a full mile long! It is a wonderful way to let the mind drift to another place in a great way, one that was a needed escape for all of us.

TRE LaVIN

I was fine on the walk through the gardens until I saw a White police officer walking with a kid who was around my age. Now the officer hadn't done anything wrong, *yet.* He was simply there to enjoy the show with someone who looked to be his son. As much as I wanted to let this go as exactly what it appeared to be, I couldn't. My dad sensed this and made sure to put himself in between me and that officer to keep me out of harm's way, real, perceived, or not.

I guess the officer could sense my uptightness. It felt like his eyes were piercing a hole through me. I couldn't shake it, that hopeless feeling of helplessness. The officer then approached my parents and spoke, saying, "First of all I am so deeply sorry for what has happened to your son and your family. I will NEVER understand the depth of your pain, being that I obviously am not a Black man." My mother was chocking back tears. The officer went on, "I just want you to know, young man, that I SEE you and YOU MATTER! As a parent and citizen first, sir, I sincerely pray that justice will be served for what happened to you all on that afternoon. We must do better. Have a good night."

My dad, who is never at a loss for words, reached out to shake that officer's hand, saying, "Thank you, sir, you really didn't have to do that. It means a lot." The officer responded, "I'm a parent. We must do more to ensure that our kids have the full opportunity not only to succeed but to live. Blessings to you all. Goodnight." His son dapped me up. I had never met them before, but I could feel his sincerity in that moment. Based on what I had experienced, I had every reason to be on edge, but kindness is a virtue, the extension of which, costs nothing but leaves me trying to escape the pool of misery that hatred has thrown me into.

As genuine as that officer and his son's gesture was, I couldn't fully receive it for what it was. Lord knows, I tried. I just couldn't. Cue, that loose-leaf:

Virtues of Kindness
Of all the things it could be...
Kindness itself is a mystery
Whose seeds are often born out of others
And a response to the depth of their misery
Why suddenly are you being

PLIGHT OF THE FORTUNATE

Friendly
Generous
Considerate
To me?
No, really and quite seriously,
Why though?
I certainly would like to know what changed
Because before right now, looking back
Kindness was an essential interpersonal skill that you lacked
Now, just like that, I'm to accept
The randomness of your non premeditated act
Why though?
The hostility and merciless hatred may not rest with you
But it continues to grip the ancestral foundation of your household
How can I be sure that you have recovered?
That your views haven't been simply
Smoothed over and covered
I want to believe you
But my innocence was compromised by the indifference
Of someone who looks just like you
I want to believe you, I really do
But I refuse to fall into the clutches of your trap
Allowing you to make pained withdrawals
Knowing that I won't be compensated properly
For deposits of virtues of kindness
That I will not soon, if ever, get back

    When Gina and my sister saw these words, they were torn. Did they really see what I saw? Weren't they there, present in the moment, also? Why was it so difficult for me to receive the simplicity of this act? Delila was initially upset with me and she let me know it when she said, "How do you ever expect to heal, Twin, if you refuse to accept the genuine kindness of others? That help has to start and come from somewhere."

    "It's not that I am refusing it, my pain just won't let receive it as openly as I used to. Officer Davis looked just as unassuming as the next guy and look what happened," I told her. Taking her hand, I continued, "Sis, I really don't know if it will ever be as simple to take others at face value ever again. As much as I want it to be the case, I'm not sure if I can get there, especially now. This is all still too fresh."

The emotion of the moment had become painfully real to Devin. He was there too, but he couldn't help but question the motive. He looked into the cop's eyes and he wanted to believe him. But the vivid picture of my head being bounced off my own car's hood left him with more questions than answers. In response he said, "Prejudice is a cancer for which there is no cure. How long are we supposed to stand by and take the mistreatment? This man may have a true heart of gold but with what you are going through Gabe, how can we know anymore?"

"We can't son," Mr. Palmer said. Looking at his wife, he continued, "And that is the part, above all else, that scares me. We won't always be able to protect him, and worse, we don't have the assurances that we will be able to protect ourselves." Just like that, in a flash, the mood changed, and a dim cloud fell over us amid the great expanse of bright lights. We managed to salvage the night, but it was a challenge.

Christmas Day came with little fanfare. Even though I was in a scattered mental place, I was still grateful for my family and crew and all the support they continued to provide. I knew that I hadn't been the easiest person to deal with, but everyone hung right in with me. With this being the case, I wrote Gina the following letter:

Dear Gina,

Merry Christmas, Love! Thank you doesn't suffice but let me start with that. I know that this part of our journey has been difficult. Certain things we shouldn't have to deal with at 17. I just want you to know how proud I am to be your boyfriend, especially knowing that being with me throughout this storm has taken so much out of you. But you really are strong, and I appreciate not only the fact that you love me, but especially how you do it. You are a beautiful young lady with a soul that is even more so.

I'm extremely excited that we will have the opportunity to continue our journey together up in Boulder at CU. I have no doubt in my mind that you will do wonderful things as you learn to spread your wings and realize the vision of what is truly possible. As you knock down barriers and walls, I stand ready, willing, and able to help you swing the hammer and the ax! It is great to see how driven you are to succeed and make your dreams come true.

Other than life itself and my family, you are the greatest gift in my life, and I am quite simply grateful for your presence and support. The present looks dark now but with you by my side there is great reason to be excited about our future. It really is about to be us against the world, and I wouldn't have that any other way. I can think of worse ways to start my day than hearing your voice. I am committed to doing all I can to make sure that doesn't change. Thank you for loving me. Keep smiling Beautiful!

Loving you from 3 houses down and beyond,

Gabriel

I stopped by her house Christmas morning to make sure that I could put that letter in her hand before we all headed to church. As I left her house, Devin was pulling up to our house. He had something for Delila, and he couldn't wait to give it to her but when she didn't answer her phone, he got worried and came straight over. "Everything is fine, Bro," I told him, trying my best to be reassuring. "Y'all can't be scaring me like that, I have something for my girl, I just wanted to hit her up before church," he told me as he reset himself.

In a move that was so 1990's, Dev put together a playlist of his and Delila's favorite songs and wanted her to listen to some of them before we left for church. She was down to do so, but she made sure to call him out for being extra corny. Devin didn't care though as he said, "Say what you want, but know that nobody is EVER going to be prouder to be your man than I am! Period! Merry Christmas!" That bit of self-assurance gave us all a laugh that we desperately needed.

The rest of the day was uneventful, as was the close to 2016. In many respects, none of us could wait to flip the calendar and turn the year over. Our families would've normally had a huge New Year's Eve party but not this year. Instead, we all just got together quietly at the Palmers house and did the best we could to enjoy one another's company.

Once 2017 was rung in, we turned our attention to MLK Day and the march to the State Capitol. The petitions were still being circulated and the response had been enormous to this point. Devin set a goal to get 15,000 signatures before the march. By January 9th, one week before the march, over 30,000 signatures had been obtained, which was no small feat. The bigger concern, looking at the upcoming forecast, was that snow was expected on the day of the march, itself.

Denver normally holds a Martin Luther King, Jr. Day "Marade," which is a cross between a parade and a march to honor Dr. King's legacy and continue to bring awareness to the struggle for equality in a nonviolent manner. On this morning, temperatures hovered around 32 degrees with 3-5 inches of snow expected. What should have deterred us and the crowd that assembled, didn't. Despite the weather, we were more resolute than ever knowing that city officials may have expected that we wouldn't come out in great number. But they were wrong. Using the annual nature of the marade as a catalyst people still came out to the tune of about 25,000.

For all intents and purposes, the march went off without any major disruptions or negativity. The peaceful nature that was envisioned at the start was realized after all. We really did use strength in numbers to bring power to the voice of our convictions as a community. Part of me didn't want to go and march that day but I knew that was not an option, given that so many people had sacrificed their valued time and energy to show up on behalf of me and my family. The turnout was encouraging for all involved, but especially for Devin. What he saw that day in the face of elements, meant to deter and work against us, was something that would aid him greatly moving forward.

I didn't speak when it was time to on the advice of my parents and others. People wanted to hear from me still, especially because they hadn't heard me speak on the matter since it happened but those who knew how to navigate this sort of thing advised me not to do so. "We'll let these signatures and petitions speak for you and for us Gabriel. We will not turn this into a dog and pony show just to satisfy someone else and their curiosities," my mother made sure to tell me.

PLIGHT OF THE FORTUNATE

Words spoken by Dr. King back in 1964 held great significance now. While speaking to students at Oberlin College, Dr. King said, "The time is always right to do what is right." It held great weight during the Civil Rights Movement when it was originally spoken and was especially poignant now. In Mr. Richardson's estimation, "It didn't matter what had been done wrong before us, what mattered was that it was still wrong today, and we were in a position to fix it to keep the same atrocities from taking place tomorrow."

We all knew that what he said was going to be easier said than done to accomplish. But with the turnout that showed up today in the snow, ice, and freezing temperatures, Mr. Palmer thought we may have the necessary ingredients to freeze out certain injustices moving forward. As a matter of warning, Mr. P. said this, "We have done a lot to prepare for this moment. We are here! We have shown up to be counted and heard." He paused before continuing, "City officials are certain that we won't sustain this momentum. It is up to us to prove them wrong. In many respects, the real work begins tomorrow after the crowd leaves and people get back to what is their comfort level of normalcy."

As much as I had been uneasy about much of what happened leading up to this day, once we got rolling, those feelings left. I got reconnected to the hope that had long since left me. Though my grip on that hope was not the strongest, I had my hands on it at least. Seeing this, my parents were going to do all they could to make sure that I didn't let go of it. Officer Davis would not go to trial for a few months, still, yet. That being the case, we knew the importance of small victories in the interim and the significance of what transpired today was not lost on any of us.

Our eighteenth birthdays would come and go. With a cloud hanging over that still had us figuratively standing in puddles of rain and tears without the aid of handkerchiefs and umbrellas I really began to understand why adults say that certain days and occasions only register as regular "days" in the grand scheme as they get older. For me especially, this "monumental" occasion had me coping more with depression than embracing celebration.

Our families tried desperately to reset. The adults took a much-needed weekend getaway to Colorado Springs to take

TRE LaVIN

in the spectacle that is the Garden of the Gods and get in some hiking and rock climbing to boot. On the adults weekend away the rest of us did some things throughout the city together that allowed us to reconnect to things that were fun and exciting to do. One of the things we made sure to do was hit Elitch Gardens, the local water and amusement park in the city.

Truth be told, I had to give myself a much-needed self-preservation talk and remember some of the baseline things that my therapist continued to remind me of, as I was still in counseling. By now, however, I was beginning to cope a little better with the circumstances that surrounded the events of the previous October. Plus, my crew was determined that we would ALL have a great time and be able to build a new set of positive memories together.

During our great adventure to Elitch's I laughed a lot more than I had in recent memory and it flowed well and came easy too. The gleam in Gina's eyes had returned, which was a welcome sight being that the light had been replaced by the overwhelming darkness of hurt while standing by my side throughout this ordeal. Devin and Delila were in rare form cracking jokes in an easy-going manner that had been absent for quite some time.

Next up was a moment in time we had all been looking forward to but hadn't been able to take stock in, our Senior Prom. It was the last major event of our high school lives that would take place before graduation. We really wanted to make this time special and were determined to do just that. Our parents wanted this for all of us even more than we did. After seeing how much we couldn't enjoy, they just wanted us to finish strong. Mrs. Richardson said it best, as she reasoned, "This is about rediscovering that which was snatched, never lost. Finish on your terms. On this night, control your happy."

This night just meant more. Period. Devin, Delila, Gina, and I had been through more in seven months than most. For our classmates, after the ACT and SAT, the biggest concern was trying to avoid getting a big pimple before the Homecoming Dance or whatnot. Not many, I doubt very seriously, had to deal with the stigma of being racially profiled and having people make excuses for the juvenile nature of their treatment. Most people can hide behind a figurative mask that will cover the truth of how they really feel. Officer Davis put his hatred for my people on full display. He wore his ignorance like a badge of (dis)honor, while I was forced to wear the shame of what he did to me like an ugly, winding scar.

We had the usual buildup ahead of the dance. The course was expertly set for a memorable night by our parents. The girls were looking amazing. Everyone came together and cooked us an amazing meal that consisted of a surf and turf theme. We would've normally gone to the after prom but decided against it, knowing how important this time together would be. When we finished eating, the limo arrived to pick us up. The ride over to the venue was surreal because we knew that time was running out for us to make anymore memories together as high schoolers.

We were able to lock in and focus on one another and enjoy the festivities. We laughed. We line danced, did the Electric Slide, the Cupid Shuffle, and the Wobble. The energy in the place was amazing. However, the most special moment of the night came when the deejay played Patti LaBelle's "If Only You Knew."

True to of the lyrics in the song, I had rehearsed what I would say to Gina but when the time came, the words didn't. I had thought about so many of the moments and memories we shared and because of Officer Davis I was forced to imagine her not being there with me. In this moment, I was glad I wasn't living in a world of fantasy knowing how much I really did need her, given all the changes that I had gone through. That song not only summed up the night but also the relationships of Gina and myself, along with Devin and my sister. We had all been through a lot and it was fitting that we were able to freeze the power of this moment together.

Over the next three weeks Vitamin C's song "Graduation (Friends Forever)" got a lot of play around school. All the questions about the uncertainty of the future would cross all our minds. Knowing our lives would change didn't seem to be the issue, it was knowing that we would never get the time to simply just be students and enjoy life without the pressures of adulthood that were certain to come.

We were set to graduate on Thursday, May 25, 2017 up at the

TRE LaVIN

Denver Coliseum. We were all excited and looking forward to what the summer would bring. In college, the four of us would be separated from day-to-day access to each other for certain functions but we knew we were only a phone call or a 40-minute drive from each other if we really needed to support one another and physically be there. All of that would take care of itself, but to no one's surprise at this point, the mood would be tempered first thing graduation morning by breaking news.

At 8:45 am my dad, who was already at the firm came home immediately to let us know what he was hearing. He told everyone to drop everything and meet him at our house. More importantly, he told us to cut off our phones and not talk to anyone but each other until he could make it back to see us all face to face. The urgency in his voice was telling, especially since graduation was less that eight hours away. What could be so important that he made us all stop EVERYTHING? We would have less that ten minutes before we would find out.

Once my dad got in the house everyone was already waiting. He said, "Listen, there is breaking news regarding Officer Davis. He will be going to trial starting Monday, June 5th. The trial, itself, is supposed to last for around two weeks with opening arguments, evidence presentations, and closing arguments." My mom's mouth dropped immediately. Amid the shock she said, "We have been waiting all this time and now he is going to trial during summer vacation. Once again, this idiot is indirectly dictating the course of action for all of us. I really hope he gets his."

My dad had delivered the news, but everyone was still confused wondering what all this really meant. Mrs. Palmer asked, "So, Andrew, why have us shut off the phones and only talk to one another? That part is puzzling." Dad was in full lawyer mode now. He made sure that he had everyone's full attention before he spoke next, saying, "I wanted to have time to prepare everyone for what we may face, especially over the next two weeks as we prepare for this trial because, I will be serving as the people's representative in what is being termed, the People vs. Charleston Davis."

"Wow, okay, then! We might finally be on the way to getting something done and justice served," Mr. Richardson said, excited. Delila chimed in next, asking, "Daddy, I know you are great at what you do, but can we really expect that this officer is going to get his issue? We all know Gabe didn't deserve what happened to him, but do we really believe that this guy will get what he *deserves*?" Agreeing with my sister, I said, "Those are great questions dad. How confident can we be in the answers?"

Dad was prepared, as he said, "Well, Gabriel, the thing that helps us here is that we have multiple eyewitnesses and camera phone footage that will fill in a lot of the blanks for us. Having that should lessen the defense's ability to find wiggle room and loopholes." We were all swept over with a great sense of relief as it finally looked like we would be getting some long-awaited answers.

Now that we had received this news and had a way forward, we were able to fully turn our attention to our graduation. The first thing we all did was head out to lunch so that we could really begin to enjoy the day ahead and the special joys that were associated with it. We really did have a great time. It really helped to know that Officer Davis would finally be heading to trial. Sitting at lunch I was overcome with emotion. This was finally happening. I couldn't fully grasp the enormity of it, but this moment had been a long time coming.

Later that evening, the four of us took the long walk across the stage to receive our diplomas. We made it. The first three laps of this journey were a cakewalk in comparison to the last one. But to have accomplished this in the face of so much adversity made me appreciate it that much more. I may have needed a little more help to get across the line, but it was better to pass the baton than to get run off the track entirely. As we all waited for the trial to start, a man's freedom wasn't the only thing on the line, so was the collective legacy of not only my family but of generations of a group of people still a long way from something that had been promised decades before; freedom and the right to be seen and treated equally.

Jen

Trial For Error

I should've been enjoying summer vacation but instead I was stuck. Stuck carrying the weight of uneven perceptions. Depending on whose opinion was being sought, I was either someone who was truly a victim of a deep seeded crime of hatred or someone who people were trying to find fault with because there was not supposed to be any conceivable way that I didn't deserve the treatment I received. Certainly, a young Black male must've been doing something wrong. Of course, the officer in question and his actions couldn't simply just be wrong. Emotions that I hadn't touched in a while were bursting back to the surface as this trial was set to begin.

Officer Davis was facing trial for excessive force with intent to injure, discriminatory harassment, conducting a discriminatory traffic stop, and attempting to stop witnesses from executing their First Amendment right to record an officer during a traffic stop. I wasn't exactly sure what that all meant. It sounded like a lot, but my dad warned us that there was a real possibility that Officer Davis wouldn't do a lot of time, even if convicted. Why? Because this case was being framed as one dealing with harassment and not the deeper issue of what it really was, that being police brutality.

I knew what I did, and I knew what I didn't do. I knew what I felt, and I also knew that a lot of those same feelings still made no sense. It was one thing to be profiled because of how I looked and what I was driving. It was something else, entirely to be treated like a pinata and tossed around like a rag doll with no regard for me as a human being. The worst part of this was that Officer Davis hadn't said anything that even remotely sounded like an apology. All he did was hide behind a bland statement that allowed him to resign.

Officer Davis may have lost his career but in many ways, he tried to take something from me before I ever had the chance to build one of my own. His actions could've stifled my growth and potential and, in some ways, did just that but there was high probability that that may not even matter and may not be enough to make the people selected for the jury even care.

Of the twelve people selected for this jury, three were Black, one was Hispanic, and eight were White. There were seven women and five men. We had hoped for more racial balance, but it was what it was. When it came to reaching a verdict, we needed people who were intelligent and unafraid to be competent in the rationale of utilizing common sense to ensure that this punishment, if there was to be one, above all, made sense. That was going to be an uphill climb and more likely, easier said than done but we had a lot of known entities on our side. Now it was time to see how everything was set to play out.

I had my doubts about showing up to the court room and watching the trial from inside. But my dad said it would be important for people to see my face and to bring truth to the harshness of what some people had only been able to speculate about until now. It was decided that all our families would go and sit in an area of the courtroom where the jury would have no choice but to acknowledge the depth of our pain even if for most of them there was absolutely no way that they could understand it.

Sure, the injustice that took place on that afternoon happened to me but in a deeper sense what happened to me happened to all of us as a people. I was not standing alone. We were standing together. Malcolm X said it best when he said, "When 'I' is replaced with 'we' even illness becomes wellness." We needed to be made whole. We needed to recover from the disease of injustice and find a cure to sustain the good of humanity.

Officer Davis's actions that day were not smart, and they were not funny by any stretch. In some strange way this trial and its lead up had become some glorified media circus. I couldn't help but think on something else Malcolm X said, while I was trying to grab hold of my feelings in this situation. The quote by Malcolm that I kept coming back to goes like this, "A wise man can play the part of a clown, but a clown can't play the part of a wise man." Over the next couple of weeks, the narrative that was going to be painted would go a log way to determining how Officer Davis and I would be viewed. I just hoped that airbrush and smokescreens wouldn't leave something that was supposed to be so clear to be viewed by everyone else through the prism of cracked lenses.

When we arrived at the courthouse there was a wave of television cameras, news reporters and journalists spread throughout the grounds. My family was escorted inside by an armed security detail. I had watched coverage of many trials on television but had never actually been in a courtroom myself, which to many people was surprising because of my dad's occupation. So, I really wasn't sure what to expect once we got inside.

Once inside though, I got a surprise that I certainly was not expecting. I was looking down at my phone when Gina and my mother both elbowed me at the same time. Startled, I said, "Ouch, what did I do?" Gina, whispered, "Nothing Gabe, but you may want to look up." As I did, I was shocked to see the officer from the Botanic Gardens. He came over and found a seat on the row behind us. Speaking to my mother and then looking at me he said, "A lot of people think I'm here for Davis, but they would be wrong." As he pointed in the direction of the defense counsel he said, "I'm not here for them, Gabriel, I am actually here for you. I wanted to lend my support to you and your family."

My mom was just as puzzled as I was as she said, "That is mighty brave of you considering the circumstances." As she adjusted in her seat, she asked the officer, "Aren't you worried about backlash and repercussions from your colleagues and co-workers?" His answer was telling. Very confidently he stated, "Actually no I'm not. Wrong is wrong. There is no way to deny or sugarcoat that fact. I wanted to be here, firsthand, to see justice served for this reprehensible behavior. Unfortunately, I don't know that it will be, but I'm hopeful." Maybe this guy and his motives were genuine after all because he certainly didn't have to show up in this setting on account of me. But he was here, walking out the action. That had to count for something.

My dad and his team came in and took their seats behind the table. He looked over to me and mouthed, "Here we go, Son, stay strong. I love you." "Love you, too," I told him. Next, Officer Davis was escorted into the courtroom. He was wearing a blue pinstriped suit and had his hands cuffed in front of him at the waist. His demeanor was decidedly different than it had been back in October. Today, he looked scared. There was a sort of emptiness in his eyes. He looked straight ahead, careful not to look over at me, as they took his legs out of the leg irons and directed him to take a seat.

Next, the bailiff told us all to rise as we awaited the arrival of Judge Sheila Adams. Dad told us that she was about her business and well respected. Coming into her courtroom, he knew to be prepared because she was inquisitive, professional, and smart. You had to be on your game because she was sure to be on hers.

As she opened the proceedings, she let all in attendance know the following:

"Good morning. As we open, I always expect order to be adhered to and maintained in my court. All evidence is expected to be presented respectfully, tactfully, and in a timely manner. Ultimately it will be up to me to determine the facts of this case and make a decision regarding said facts. Ladies and gentlemen of the jury you have been given your instructions. Counselors, are you ready to proceed?"

With a unified "Yes, Your Honor," we were set to begin. There was a high level of tense energy in the room. Anticipation had been building for a while and now the moment of truth had arrived. It was time to find out if there would be any faith left in the legal process or if we would leave with the bitter taste in our mouths that had been the company of so many people that had been wronged before us, who in many ways, were still in search of vindication and justice.

Opening arguments started things off. Of course, Officer

Davis was portrayed as an upstanding citizen who had been a decorated member of the police force. He was lauded for the medals and commendations that he had received. This situation was framed as being an exception rather than the rule. His lawyer told the jury of the set of negative circumstances that he endured in the two months prior to the traffic stop and how him having a "setback" put him in the frame of mind to act the way that he did on that October afternoon.

My dad was all over this when it was his turn to speak. He questioned why Officer Davis had been found fit to be on duty that day given the fact that he was going through such a hard time that led to this "setback." My dad argued that Officer Davis was not going through a setback. Instead, my dad argued that this traffic stop was just a glorified way to let his supreme level of arrogance show and that negative circumstances were not what Officer Davis was suffering from at all. My dad offered that Officer Davis acted as if he was above the law and he didn't account for the strength of the community showing up and the power of restraint that they showed once they arrived. Because of the people being unafraid to exercise their First Amendment rights, Officer Davis now had to account for the one thing that had alluded him well before this incident but especially since, the truth.

Dad went through the next four days calling different eyewitnesses and getting them to testify to what they saw on that day. The defendant's legal counsel cross examined hoping to discredit any and everything that the witnesses said. As week one of the trial wrapped, the judge reminded everyone of what was at stake here and warned everyone of the media scrutiny and presence surrounding the case and how we all needed to be careful because there were vultures circling who just wanted to get their hands on an exclusive so that they would be able to profit off of the notoriety of our collective anguish and misfortune.

The next Monday we were all back in court so that the defense could present their side of the case. All kinds of character witnesses were brought forth to speak of the type of man that Officer Davis was away from the job. They tried to soften his image by spotlighting the type of husband and father that he was and how active he had been in the community up to that day. They also tried to speak to the level of remorse that had come over him in the months since and what he had done to try to become a better man.

The entire ordeal was exhausting. When it came time for Officer Davis to speak, he exercised his Fifth Amendment rights. This angered a lot of people who thought that he should have to face questioning about what he did and explain himself. Without being able to hear from the man himself, it was difficult to get a read on the jurors to see how they might be leaning. We would have another weekend to sit through before closing arguments gave way to Officer Davis's fate being handed off to the jury. On Monday, June 19th, the jury went into deliberations to reach a verdict. At 1:30 pm on that afternoon the jury was officially put on the clock. As this process began my emotions got put through the wringer because I was fully in touch with all I had felt throughout this ordeal but even worse, I was overcome with fear and doubt that somehow this guy was about to get away with what he did to me and be able to walk free.

On Wednesday, the 21st at 10:05 am we were all called back into the courtroom because the jury had reached a verdict. Hearing that, I almost passed out. My parents made sure to warn us that a verdict is only part of the process. If, and my mom used *if* very carefully, there was a guilty verdict we couldn't rest on those laurels. The sentencing itself would tell the true story.

See, as an example, a person can be sentenced based on a range of time. The minimum punishment for something may carry a five-year sentence mandate, while the maximum may be *up to* 25 years. That paints an overly broad brush that doesn't guarantee that a person will spend anywhere near the full amount of time behind bars that they are sentenced to and they may not have to serve the minimum amount of time sentenced either. They told me this so that I would be prepared. They also told all of us that whatever the verdict was would incite a lot of different emotions for people depending on what side of the fence they found themselves on.

As we waited for the judge to come in, I saw something that brought tears to my eyes, though I wasn't the first one to be moved to tears. Devin spotted two White women wearing t-shirts with a hashtag on them that read, "#Justice4Gabriel." It wasn't the hashtag that caught us off guard, it was the fact that White people were the ones wearing the t-shirts with the message on them in the first place. What this gesture, coupled with the actions of the officer from the Botanic Gardens, showed was that this incident lit the flame of rage under people who saw a threat levied against the very foundation of the human condition.

These women got the point. That officer and his son from the Gardens got the point. But there was still a bigger question that needed to be answered. Would the people on the jury get the point? I didn't know. My parents didn't know. Neither did Devin or Gina's families. None of us knew that answer. Truth be told that uncertainty is what scared us most. Sympathy didn't seem to be an issue here. Anyone can feel sorry for another person. Empathy, on the other hand, was the thing that seemed to really be in question. Could other people who didn't have to live the truth of being Black in America every day truly *empathize* with the foundational piece of our struggle? Through this verdict we were about to find out.

Judge Adams came in and once she was seated, the jury followed. "Have you all reached a verdict?" she asked. "Yes, Your Honor," the jury foreman said in response. You could feel the tension in the courtroom now. "Would the defendant please stand?" the judge asked Officer Davis. Once Officer Davis stood, he faced the jury and readied to hear his fate.

The foreman was ready. She stood up and read the following:

"Regarding the following charges against the defendant, Mr. Charleston Mark Davis we the jury have reached the following conclusions. Regarding count # 1, excessive force with intent to injure, we the jury find the defendant, guilty." My mother started to cry. "Regarding count # 2, discriminatory harassment" the foreman stated, "We the jury find the defendant, guilty." Gina was squeezing my hand. As we readied for the final two verdicts to be read, Devin draped his hands on my shoulders. My mom was rubbing the small of my back.

There was a deafening quietness that fell over the room. "Regarding count # 3, conducting a discriminatory traffic stop," the foreman continued, "We the jury find the defendant, guilty." Delila stepped around to embrace me as the final verdict was read. Lastly, the foreman concluded, "Regarding count # 4, attempting to stop witnesses from executing their First Amendment right to record an officer during a traffic stop, we the jury find the defendant, guilty." My dad looked skyward and could only manage to raise his hands in total submission to the Lord above.

Andrew Clarkson had a sterling legal record in the courtroom, having won 92% of his cases over time. He never went into a case expecting to lose. Yet, given some of the ways that different verdicts have turned out with police brutality and misconduct as the culprit, he wasn't totally confident that the verdict itself would go in our favor. In hearing this verdict, he wasn't celebrating this victory as a lawyer. He was celebrating this victory as a father and husband who had watched his family go through a hell that nobody should ever have to experience.

Delila was completely overcome with emotion. It had been hard at different times along this journey to watch me go through the trials and tribulations that were evoked throughout. In this moment, though, accountability took on a totally different meaning. Once the jury reiterated that the verdict that was read was indeed one that was fair and true, Officer Davis was handcuffed, taken into custody, and led out of the courtroom. In the next 60 days he would be sentenced.

As the courtroom was washed over in pure relief and jubilation I looked around and took in the beauty of what just happened. I knew that this verdict was only part of the process but for the first time since this event took place and altered the course of my life, I was able to experience the satisfaction of knowing that I would be okay.

A press conference was held on the steps of the courthouse 30 minutes after the verdict was read. It had taken eight long, tedious, and overwhelming months to go from being forcibly stood up to being able to triumphantly stand up. My parents spoke to the press and then I was able to make a statement, though I wouldn't take any questions afterword. When the time came, I stepped confidently to the podium and said:

"I am forever grateful to my family and the people of this great community who stood up and took what happened to me personal. What began as a simple trip to the grocery store turned into much more and it feels good to know that the person that did these things to me is now being forced to take true accountability for his actions. Thank you."

As much as I wanted to speak at length, I was directed to keep my remarks short so that people wouldn't be pulling at me unnecessarily. Though I made my statement, there was so much more depth to what I felt. Looking around at the group of people that had supported me through it all I was genuinely happy to know that they were in my corner. As we made it to the car to head home, I wept openly and uncontrollably. I had kept so much bottled up and it was a relief to be able to let everything out.

When we made it home there was so much that I wanted to do but everything was put on hold because I was exhausted. We all were. I laid down to rest and was surprised that I ended up sleeping for 4 hours straight. This was significant because since this ordeal took place, I hadn't been able to sleep for more than two hours at a time without being awakened for a handful of different reasons. I came to find out later that one of the reasons my body was unable to rest was because my soul was grieved and uncomfortable. I woke up refreshed and ready to explore what was next. I had about two months before I was due to start college and I was determined to enjoy them.

Even with that being the case, we didn't do much over that time, but we did a lot to decompress. I spent a lot of time out at Ferril Lake with Gina just talking about the future and enjoying the person that I was going to spend it with. It was much of the same for Devin and my sister. Before we could close this chapter of the story however, you know we had to throw one last party... and we had to make sure we did it big too.

Eleven

College Bound, Trouble Found

Officer Davis wound up getting sentenced to eight years in prison for the crimes that he committed against me. Once we found that out, our families wanted to have one last celebration to spotlight how far we had all come and find a way to look forward to the future. We would throw a block party. I thought this would be appropriate given how much the community stood with us throughout our ordeal. It just felt right. There would be music, food, and fellowship, all the ingredients that make a Clarkson party uniquely special.

We had inflatables, popcorn machines, ice cream, snow cones, a scavenger hunt, face painting, and relay races. So many people came out, lending their continued support, wanting to wish us well as we moved on to the next part of our collective journey. We knew most of the people in our neighborhood, but this turnout was beyond amazing. It really felt good to have everyone come together in this way.

We had a 1980's theme for our party. People came dressed as Earth, Wind, and Fire, Michael Jackson, Prince, Lisa Lisa, and Cult Jam, Whodini, Tina Turner, and New Edition to name a few. We got special approval to have a firework show and there were even people navigating the street on roller skates. This was a special moment worthy enough to be frozen in time, if only that could've been the case.

TRE LaVIN

Devin and I took a walk and reminisced about the great times we had growing up together and what it meant for us to be embarking on this next phase of our lives moving forward. He told me not to worry about my sister because he would make sure that she was taken care of. He asked me very sincerely to take good care of Gina because the last four years provided him with the sister her never had, in her. We knew this wasn't a goodbye because we were only going to be a short trip up the interstate from each other, but there was still some form of finality to this moment. We literally had spent almost everyday around each other since age 11 when he moved here from California. He truly had become family to us, he, and his parents. We wouldn't have had it any other way.

As we were taking our walk, Delila and Gina were taking theirs. Since they were 4th graders these two had been inseparable. The power of this moment was not lost on them. They shed a lot of tears as they took a walk down memory lane. Gina made sure to let Delila know how much I and my sister meant to her. She said that Delila wasn't just her friend, she was truly the sister she never had. Delila said that as long a she could remember all her benchmark moments involved Devin, Gina, myself, or our families. It was going to be different not seeing each other daily but the girls knew that the other would be in great hands because of Devin and me.

There was one bit of warning that Delila did have for Gina and that was to look out for me and help protect me from myself, especially given my negative history with trauma. "D, listen, I have been right here with you, your brother, and your family every step of the way and that won't change now. I love that man and I wouldn't be able to live with myself if something happened to him," Gina told my sister. "That's why I love you, girl," Delila said, unafraid to let the tears flow in response.

The DU campus is beautiful. As Devin and Gina embarked on their collegiate journey together, they were enamored by the architectural beauty of the campus itself. Byron Theatre, Newman Center for the Performing Arts, and Gates Concert Hall would become a home away from home for Delila. Even though our parents lived less than five miles and fifteen minutes from campus, Dev and my sister decided to live on campus so that they could get the full college experience. They would come to call Johnson-McFarlane Hall (J-Mac) home early on.

As they settled in on campus, it was not uncommon to find them at the Jelly U Café with Delila getting lost in the lavender blueberry pancakes and Devin finding peace in the French toast. If they ever needed a rest away from everyone and everything it was not uncommon to find them here, especially since they could get breakfast there all day. Devin also has a thing for burgers and Park Burger is a place to get some of the best burgers in town. If it wasn't breakfast on his mind, you could probably catch him thinking about a burger from that spot. While Devin always seemed to be chomping at the bit for burgers, Delila could often be found craving chicken nachos, especially from Pioneer Bar near campus.

Being that Delila was a theatre major she was always looking for a place to take in live music and sit in venues where she could become one with the atmosphere. For her, there was just something fulfilling about hearing bands play live. With everything that happened to our families over the handful of months preceding college, Delila took a serious liking to blues music. Once she found Lincoln's Roadhouse that was a wrap. They are famous for their meatloaf cheeseburger (Delila's favorite) and the pot roast burrito (Devin's favorite). The live blues shows are next level. Delila found solace in being able to get lost in this atmosphere and her and Devin used opportunities as such to draw closer to one another.

Meanwhile, getting settled in at CU was going well for Gina and me too. Because I was a journalism major who was part of the college of media, communication, and information I was assigned to Buckingham Hall in the Kittredge area of campus. Gina on the other hand, was assigned to Hallett Hall because of her ethnic studies major. The dorm she was in really fostered positive dialogue that helped re-enforce the power of identity and culture for those in the Black community. Living here gave her the necessary tools for empowerment that would ultimately lead to her greatest success down the line. We also liked living on campus where we did, given the proximity of our dorms to each other, Folsom Field, and the CU Events Center.

One of the places that Gina and I found close by was a restaurant called The Sink. This spot became our go to for pizza and burgers in the area. The Slaughterhouse 5 pizza became one of our favorites given that it was loaded with five meats that we loved. It had Italian sausage, pepperoni, ground beef, Canadian bacon, and uniquely spiced chicken with mozzarella cheese sprinkled over their classic tomato sauce. The classic Sink Burger has a flavor all its own and that became a favorite of Gina's while I took a liking to the Big Bad Wolf burger with its house smoked brisket, bacon, and special Sink sauce with provolone. And not to be outdone, the mac and cheese is a true delicacy that has green onions, bleu cheese, and crispy chicken tenders to boot.

Another spot in Boulder that we couldn't get enough of was a place called Foolish Craig's Café. We really loved the food there (the Fool's Paradise three egg omelet, anyone?) but the deserts and the fresh baked goods are what kept us coming back, especially their Butter Rum Caramel Crepe Cake. On one morning, however, Gina and I got the most pleasant surprise. A baby faced looking brown haired White guy recognized me standing at the register to pay and called for me.

He looked familiar but I couldn't quite place where I knew him from. There was no mistaking the fact that he knew Gina and me though. As he began to speak, he was quiet, saying, "Excuse me, I don't mean to intrude but are you, Gabriel Clarkson?" His tone was extremely reserved, but he was attentive and respectful. "Yes, I am, but while you look familiar, please forgive me because I can't place who you are. I'm sorry," I told him.

He continued, "No worries, I completely understand. My name is Tyler Henson, you may remember me and my dad from the Botanic Gardens over Christmas and my dad from Officer Davis's trial." Gina answered first, as she said, "Tyler, it is so nice to formally meet you. Are you going to school here?" "The honor is mine," Tyler said in response. He paused before continuing, "Yeah, I'm a journalism major, I got assigned to Buckingham Hall." "Really? That's cool. I am over in Buck Hall, also, same major," I told him.

"Look, man, I want to clear something up. My dad really did show up FOR YOU. There was no ulterior motive then and there isn't one now. It absolutely broke his heart to see what that officer did to you. He was livid that there wasn't more punishment dulled out for him after the verdict. Anyway, it is nice to formally meet you two, hopefully I'll see you guys around." Tyler and I went on to exchange contact information and promised to keep in touch. Strange enough, I was at ease seeing him. It was comforting to know that his dad really was there to support me. I hated to admit it, but I had them wrong. Not all police officers are bad after all. But the one's who are, make it hell for others to do their jobs and put citizens on edge, especially not knowing if they will get a fair shake.

Being that I had now seen Tyler and his father on multiple occasions, I felt much better knowing that there was someone else from my community who shared an empathetic viewpoint. Going forward, Tyler would be someone I could lean on. We ended up having a lot more n common that I would've initially given him credit for. I was glad that was the case and Gina shared in that sentiment.

We all had settled in at college. As we did, the pact we made at the start would come to be extremely important. We all made sure to call each other every day. As we did, it helped with the adjustment we were all experiencing being away from one another. We did our best to hold each other accountable and it worked, except in one area of deep concern for me.

My dad had built a solid reputation over time and it was well earned. After what happened at the trial, that reputation had a deep and solid foundation. Dad was being looked at with the same manner of reverence that once followed Johnnie Cochran after the role he played in the acquittal of O.J. Simpson during his "Trial of the Century" back in 1995 after being put on trial for the murder of his ex-wife and her friend. Obviously, the circumstances were not the same and far from equal, but that didn't stop people from putting my dad on a makeshift pedestal. It may not have been fair, but through his representation during that trial Black people were able to reach out and touch something that had eluded us for generations. Hope.

TRE LaVIN

During business hours (9:00 am to 5:00 pm) I was fine because I had schoolwork to focus on. During those off-peak times between dusk and dawn, if I was with Gina, I was fine. However, in those times when I was isolated with my thoughts, I desperately needed something to keep me focused. Looking back on it now, honestly, I can admit that I did a horrible job of this. See, I always liked playing dominoes, cards, board games, and the like. I was rather good at them too. I had confidence that I could win most any game that I could play, especially if I understood the different intricacies and nuances of the games themselves. Most times, I was content playing for fun and the enjoying the company that came with it. But at some point, during that first semester, all of that changed.

Gina had gone back to Denver to see her mom and help her prepare for a fundraiser that she was organizing. When she left, I was in a great mental space. I had spoken to her on her ride back home and even heard from my sister in the process. Devin called and we chopped it up for a few also. Because I had a project to finish, I couldn't accompany Gina on the trip. I sat up in my dorm room, working feverishly to finish the project I was working on. I got hung up on one of the concepts and was confused as to what my next step should be.

After about ten minutes and not being able to find a relevant fix to the issue, I heard Tyler pass in the hall. I wasn't sure if he could help me, but I was going to find out. "Hey T, can you come here for a minute?" I asked him. "Sure, G give me just a second. I'll be right over after I drop this off," he let me know as he hurriedly made his way down the hall past my room. Five minutes later, he came back.

As it turns out, I only needed to make a minor tweak to my process. Once Tyler made that clear for me and explained it, I was able to put the finishing touches on what I had been working on. We decided to sit down for a minute and get to know each other a bit better. I found out that writing came easy to Tyler, but he lacked the creative nature needed to make his stuff "pop" in his estimation. He let me read some of the investigative pieces he had written while he was in high school at Thomas Jefferson High. As I was reading, there was no way to deny the gift he had. I was creative but Tyler was transformative in the way he delivered information. I learned then that we could truly be an asset to one another if we weren't threatened by the gift possessed by the other.

I also found out that he was a real fan of the actor Tim Allen and that he absolutely loved India.Arie and Earth, Wind, and Fire too. Anyone who knows anything about Denver knows that these legends have left their mark not only on our city but on the world! Sitting with him and having in depth conversation made me realize how fortunate I was to begin building a friendship with him. I apologized to him for not giving him a fair shake in the beginning and hoped that he could forgive my ignorance and stupidity. He did but he had his eyes on a bigger issue.

He asked me to hear him out. Rubbing his chin, he said, "Gabriel, I want to be able to understand what makes us different so that we can work toward finding effective ways to get on the same page as young men in this society. I want to be able to educate my White friends and show them an empathetic and educated viewpoint." I nodded. "See, I don't want to see my friends hurting and not be able to understand their why. Can you please help me? I don't just want my information to be as stale as the books that I've read from, I want to move toward a sincere and reformed outcome," he said. The tears in his eyes told a story that I wasn't ready to read but I was appreciative of the fact that he wanted to understand.

There were some old "Andy Griffith Show" reruns on. Tyler and I sat down to watch them together. I laughed in ways I never had before this moment. We established a depth of understanding, giving us a level of clarity that would not only help us become better journalists, but more importantly, better citizens. Just after 8:30 pm, Tyler headed out to make a few phone calls, leaving me to ponder everything we had discussed.

I started to doze off just after 9:15 pm. I was in a great place, having just had this conversation with Tyler. He taught me more in that moment than I had learned in a while. As I was starting to get comfortable, I heard a loud crashing outside the dorm. Someone's car had collided with one of the posts just down the walk from the dormitory entrance. Hearing that sound sent me spiraling back to a place I thought I had put in my rearview mirror. Boy, was I wrong!

I had a full-on panic attack. I was shaking uncontrollably. I couldn't get my head or my heart to stop pounding. Previously, my therapist had me draft a list of safe people that I could call if I ever got into a situation mentally that I couldn't pull myself out of on my own. I needed to activate my list, so I began making phone calls.

The people on the list all knew exactly what to say or do to give me the time and space to calm down and center myself. The problem was, however, that when I needed someone to help me through, no one picked up their phone. Not my therapist. Not my parents. Not my sister. Not Devin. Not Gina. Not their parents either. I was stuck. Not knowing what to do I tried to do something that would allow me to focus. I went downstairs to where some other students were playing poker.

My entrance into this game was simple enough. I started to calm down once I started winning. One of the guys thought I was showing him up. That wasn't the case, but there was nothing I could do to convince him. After losing four consecutive hands, he had a proposition. "Look Gabriel, why don't we make this a little more interesting? You ever play for money?" "Absolutely not! That is not something that I do, and I am not about to start now, "I told him, stern as ever. That answer didn't suffice. "The way you are playing man, you don't have anything to worry about. What's one hand?" he said, tying his best to convince me. "One hand," I told him. I didn't account for what came next. The bet was $10 each for the hand. $20 seemed harmless enough. No sweat. I didn't expect 15 other people to add $10 each to the pot. Now, suddenly, the pot had swollen to $170. Against my better judgement, I was doing the one thing I swore I never would. I was gambling.

I heard my parents recount the negativity of their ordeal from their teenage years too many times to count. I knew where they stood on the matter. I knew that there was always a possibility that good luck could run out and everything could be lost in an instant. I knew that what I was about to do could have its own set of negative consequences for me. I needed to walk away but the adrenaline rush had already taken hold. I needed someone on my list to call me back. I needed a way out. I needed an accountability partner, someone to rescue me from myself. It wasn't to be, however. My own adrenaline had medicated the symptoms of my pain. Common sense had left. I wanted to feel something, anything, that would snap me back to reality. It wasn't to be, though. I was officially numb. That adrenaline rush had become the one thing I didn't need it to be, my own worst enemy!

If my parents found out what was going on, they would have my head. I knew it too. This wasn't a good situation or place for me to be stuck in. I won the hand and more importantly, I did walk away. But the seed had been planted and the damage done. Getting the false assurance that I could overcome the negativity of what this panic attack and its affects left by getting lost in the adrenaline rush of what I was now feeling was a mistake that I was about to pay dearly for, even if the consequences of those actions would take some time to manifest.

By the time Delila called me back, morning had come. Matter of fact, I had slept so hard that I missed ten return calls from my accountability partners. The good news was that I no longer was showing signs of the panic attack that had reared its ugly head the night before. The bad news, though, was that the way I found to cope and get through was going to somehow cost me dearly. Not now in the present. Not even in the immediate future. But what was coming was going to have me in way too deep, possibly costing my family everything, including their good name.

When I spoke to Delila I filled her in on all the details of what had transpired the night before. "Twin, I know that was scary for you and I'm sorry that I didn't answer. How are you feeling, now?" she went on to ask. "I'm fine. It was scary. I was able to get some sleep," I told her. As much as I wanted to believe what I told Delila, I was lying. I wanted her to believe that I had everything under control. I wanted to believe that myself. I did manage to return all the calls that I missed. Somehow, I convinced myself that all was well. I couldn't bring myself to tell the truth about where I was mentally, so I lied, to everyone, thinking that it would make me feel better. Again, I was wrong. I felt terrible. I kept trying to justify my actions, thinking that the stench of what happened would somehow fade away. It wasn't so bad. At least that is what I kept telling myself.

Over the next few months, anytime I was overcome with anxiety, I would find a way to gamble. This didn't have a negative affect on my schoolwork. I still managed to make the Dean's List. I would return home a handful of times and fall right in line, keeping things normal and not ruffling feathers. I needed everyone to know that I was okay. I didn't want to put them through anything that remotely resembled the pain that had been on display months earlier. So, I hid it. Gina, Devin, and my sister knew I was struggling. They had no clue how much, though, and I wanted to keep it that way. So, I did all I could to keep the true depth of what had become my new normal a secret.

Twelve

It All Comes Down to This

Over the next three years my crew and I did a solid job of marketing ourselves, honing our skills, and getting better. I was building a high-end portfolio in both Boulder and Denver and Gina was doing the same. Each time the two of us returned to Denver, we were amazed at all Devin and Delila were accomplishing. They had really maximized their reach and come together to establish something tangible that was going to leave an indelible footprint. Our parents were proud as well. We were exceeding expectations and doing our part to move the legacies that our families had built forward.

Devin was building a very impressive list of contacts down at City Hall. At one point, he even managed to secure a high-profile panel discussion as part of one of the finals for a class that he was taking. Because of this, he was able to hear directly from prominent law and decision makers and really gain an understanding for the process of how certain laws and measures for reform get made. He was viewed as one of the promising, rising stars to watch.

Delila was gaining notoriety for several of her performances in the university's theatre productions. Freshman year, it was her performance as Rosie DeLeon in *Bye, Bye Birdie*. Sophomore year, she turned heads as Marian Paroo in *The Music Man*. Yet, her most powerful performance came when she played Lena Younger in *A Raisin in the Sun*. As one person put it, "Delila Clarkson owned the role of Lena Younger. In the end you couldn't help but root for her and the Younger family as this story reached its conclusion. You could tell the emotional investment that she put into her performance." This was high praise, for sure. Delila knew that she had a gift and was very good at what she did. But the praise she was receiving humbled her and left her at a loss for words.

Gina was able to obtain the services of someone to mentor her and assist her with getting her foot in the door in the Boulder community. Seeing how many children lacked certain foundational opportunities to succeed, it was really placed on her heart to become a social worker. She was able to meet people who allowed her to make need and risk assessments to determine the level of care and support she would need. In certain poverty-stricken sections of town, she was able to aid in the planning and administration of programs that brought a ground swell of support to strengthen areas where the otherwise traditional pipelines had failed.

For Gina providing a quick fix was not the answer. She wanted to ensure that solid infostructure would be in place to help overcome some of the soul wrenching heartbreak she would see when she interacted with the children and families in these communities. Above all, she wanted to be certain that the voiceless would not only have a voice but that that voice was impactful enough to shift the narrative and allow their needs to be heard and addressed. After what she witnessed in our community after what happened to me in high school, she was encouraged by what she saw. She knew that if things were presented in the proper way that mountains could be moved.

She really wanted to spearhead different community improvement programs to help residents address socioeconomic barriers and hinderances that led to so many of the negative things that hurt our communities at large. Key among those factors were underperforming schools, crime, poor health, and low property values. She just wanted to be a beacon of light in the place where she lived and ultimately have it be a place that people were proud to call home.

As for me, I had the foundational things already completed regarding my nonprofit. I had drafted the plan, written the mission statement and filed the nonprofit articles of incorporation forms. The people who would serve on my board of directors had been selected and we had our first set of meetings to discuss the bylaws and standards that we would be governed by at length. Our conflict-of-interest policy was created, and I had applied for my employee identification number (EIN). Now I just needed to apply for my exemption status.

Things really were looking up. I had a solid concept for the nonprofit. I was applying for various grants to get necessary funding. The other thing that is great to have in this situation is money. Through various contacts I had obtained up in Boulder, I found out that I may not have to do much to procure additional funds. A classmate of mine named Joshua Wright really took a liking to the nonprofit concept and idea. He introduced me to his parents, and we had a great meeting. At the meeting's conclusion they informed me that they would like to provide financial backing for the project, to the tune of $500,000. Yes, you read that right. The amount floored me too!

No one had ever taken this type of chance on me before, or anyone I knew for that matter. I wanted to know what the catch was. After speaking to Joshua and seeing how passionate he was about the project, all his parents wanted to do was meet me and get to know more about the vision that I had. Once they were able to see the vision and have it explained in detail, they had no problem extending the offer to me. As astounding as this amount was, I still didn't want to make a quick or uniformed decision so I took about two weeks to do research on the people who were set to become my silent partners so that I could be sure. I needed to get this part of the program right the first time. I heard too many horror stories about how different people mismanaged their funding and ended upside down trying to crawl out of the hole that was dug as a result.

All preliminary accounts had me feeling good about bringing them on as my silent investors. The Wrights were ecstatic about this opportunity and as the days passed so was I. Eventually, I found out that the source of the money they were offering was an illegal gambling ring that they had been running, centered on sports betting. My initial response was that I can't have anything to do with this. Yet, I was still intrigued due to the amount of money that was being offered. Where else and how else would I come up with that type of money upfront?

Given the consequences that were sure to arise out of this type of transaction, I shouldn't have had to wrestle with the decision at all. But I did and I was. Why? Because since my flashback and traumatic experience dating back to my freshman year at CU, anytime I found myself struggling I sought out comfort in playing card games and such for money. I had managed to garner a solid reputation around the city too, especially with the underground crowd. Whenever I wasn't on a hot streak, I wouldn't stick around too long to keep trying my luck. So, I didn't really see what I was doing as an issue because I didn't owe anybody anything. I had no debt on anybody's books.

But now I had this offer on the table. I knew I had to turn it down. But the struggle was real. Katharine Hepburn said it best when she said, "If you obey all the rules, you'll miss all the fun." Most of my life, I had done nothing but follow the rules. In doing so, I witnessed many people taking shortcuts and still finding ways to get ahead. That can be frustrating because at times, it seems that those working the hardest are also having to work the longest to get ahead.

I was doing the right thing when Officer Davis stopped me, and it didn't make a difference. He still was able to do what he wanted to do to me. Ultimately, justice was served but it still didn't stop him from thinking it was okay to do what he did and even worse, carry it out. The Wrights believed in what I was doing and wanted to help. Where is the harm in that? When someone can help, shouldn't a person in need take the offering? I knew the correct answer but by now I was sort of growing tired of being a docile rule follower. I wanted to win at something else for a change.

My family and Gina still didn't know about this offer and what was being presented. I knew that once I made them aware of the situation, the answer I got back in return wouldn't be something that I wanted to hear. $500,000 is a lot of money and having that amount at my disposal would put me in lines and open doors that wouldn't otherwise be open, especially so early in the process.

PLIGHT OF THE FORTUNATE

Before I could talk to my parents, Delila, Gina, and Devin to get their thoughts, I knew I had to talk to Joshua and his parents first.

I had requested to meet with the Wrights after classes before my weekend was to begin. They were happy to address my concerns. Above all, they wanted to be sure that we were all on the same page. I thanked them for their belief in me and let them know how appreciative I was for their valued time and for even considering such an investment in the first place, especially given that, for all intents and purposes, I was an unproven commodity.

I was shaking a little, with sweaty palms as I began speaking to Mrs. Wright. I said, "Ma'am, while I greatly appreciate the kindhearted nature of your family's gesture, I'm not sure that I can accept this money." Mr. Wright was thoroughly confused as he stood up, saying, "So, you are ready to walk away from $500,000? Just like that? That seems a little odd, what changed?" In response I managed to say, "With all due respect, sir, in doing my research I found that your family was involved in some illegal activities and I just feel that it is best for me to steer clear." I was giving myself a hug trying to calm down.

Mr. Wright was laughing. Mrs. Wright was just shaking her head in disbelief. Through his chuckling, Mr. Wright looked at his wife and said, "You hear that Linda? This young man seems to think our money isn't good. Like its tainted or something." Still shaking her head, she said, "Oh yeah, I heard him!" "You know, its funny," Mr. Wright continued, "Two weeks ago, the prospect of taking our money wasn't a problem. But now it is. What? Are we not entitled to make money how we choose? The life I provide for my family renders no complaints." Mrs. Wright seemed to have had enough when she said, "Here we are offering you an opportunity to build wealth and a fortune, one where you don't have to struggle out of the gate, and this is what you come back to us with? Don't forget, just as easy as it is to offer this piece of heaven, it is so much easier to turn your life into a living hell! Choose wisely."

The were scaring me now. They didn't have to do what they were attempting to do. But, I didn't expect this type of response. Most people, when backed into a corner like that, will try to lie to cover up something they are not doing right. This situation, however, was just the opposite. They weren't denying that they were apart of the illegal gambling scene. But they were taking offense to the fact that I couldn't use their money because of *how they got it.* They told me to seriously reconsider my decision. Despite how I was feeling, they still wanted to provide funding for me. "Take a month to think it over Gabriel, but give us an answer soon," Mr. Wright told me.

As much as I wanted to, I couldn't tell my inner circle about what was going on. I knew I needed to, but I couldn't. Not yet. I needed to be sure. The one person who did know what was going on was Tyler. He thought that I should take the money, initially anyway, but he didn't know my parents' story and why they wouldn't approve. Once I told him, he started to sound a lot like them in his reasoning. "There is no way you can do this Gabriel. I know that this is a life changing amount of money and it would do so much to help you accomplish your dream and give life to it, but there are just too many variables," he told me, deeply concerned now.

The fact that he was sounding so much like my parents agitated me. It really did and I couldn't hide it. "Don't you understand, Tyler, opportunities like this just don't come out of thin air," I told him. There was hurt in his eyes as he started pleading with me, saying, "Look, Gabriel, I feel where you are coming from. I am not concerned as much about the thin air as I am about the ground and this family's ability to put you six feet deep if something goes wrong here. You know they are connected to the underground world, but do you know how connected they are? That is reason for concern."

I wrestled with my decision to take the money or not for the entirety of the next month. The back and forth of my own indecision was wearing me out. If I told the Wrights no, how could I be sure that I would ever get this close to money like this again in one singular transaction? I wasn't sure and I didn't know. For me, that made everything about this feel worse. My mind should've been made up by this time but it wasn't. I was still trying to justify all the reasons that this could work. But was it really going to be worth it to lose my family, as I was certain I was going to after I told them about this offer.

PLIGHT OF THE FORTUNATE

Over the last handful of years, I struggled greatly with my faith. I knew God was my source but coming out the other side of that traffic stop made me wonder often where God was amid all this chaos. I even wondered once if he truly did exist because for a long stretch, nothing seemed to be going right for me, my family, or my friends. Now, with this new development involving the Wrights, I was struggling with a certain sense of entitlement. With everything that did happen to me, I felt like I deserved the opportunity to finish first. I really did and there was not much anyone was going to do that would help change my mind.

Time was passing rather quickly in the grand scheme of things. Getting ready to return home for spring break of what is now my senior year of college has forced me to look back and consider everything that has brought me and those I care about to this point. I was genuinely excited to be coming back home, knowing that I only had about five weeks until college graduation. Before I could do that, however, I had one piece of important business to tend to. I asked Joshua to talk to his parents so I could meet with them and inform them of my decision. As hard as it was to do this, I decided that I wouldn't take their money. Telling them this didn't sit well as they didn't take kindly to being denied and turned down, but it was the right thing to do for all involved.

Gina and I headed home. We were looking forward to a week spent back in our neighborhood. Everything was falling into place for a bright future for the two of us doing things that we were truly passionate about. I was looking forward to spending some time in the park at the lake so that I could sit and release some words from my soul onto my favorite brand of loose leaf. Once we got home, Devin and Delila decided to come and meet Gina and me in the park so that we could catch up. We wanted to meet with our parents to discuss plans for the summer and possible internships after we graduated. Gina and I would be relocating back to the city and in doing so the four of us decided that we would start looking for homes of our own very near to one another, and hopefully in the same neighborhood. We wanted to continue to build on the legacy and add our own footprints by continuing to walk out our life's journey together. This, we all knew was a necessary component to writing this very impactful part of our history.

    Gina had made such a lasting impact on me. Watching her growth up close during our college years was a wonderful source of inspiration for me. I was so happy to see how things were turning out for her and I was glad to be a part of it all. To express my deep sense of gratitude for her, while in the park, I wrote this:

Reason
This fight is no longer fair
and the thing is, I know how much you care
being that you've already shifted my world and stared
a searing and impactful hole through my worn soul
recalling memories that have forced me to low crawl
back to the remnants of my deeply cracked existence
and search the very part of me that only you could make whole
well, you and God anyway...
because in Him and in you I found a new reason,
one that transcends
the vast landscapes of seasons, space, and time...
one that marks occasions with tears that I've cried
and provides a reservoir calm enough for me to swim...
and though I never learned to swim, actually,
I will allow you to be my lifeguard and God to be my lifeline...
because going forward I don't want to live with two things:
regret and resentment, even knowing I could drown
it will all be worth it...
looking back, and seeing that I did it with you, my queen
Finding gems worthy of you is my only hope now
to sit atop your head, and sparkle as part of your crown

    After hearing this, my entire crew was in tears. It was great to be able to share this space with them once again. We headed to my house ready to eat, fellowship, and discuss the excitement of our futures with our parents. The sounds of Earth, Wind, and Fire greeted us at the door, so we already knew the type of mood they were all in. Everyone was laughing, joking, and carrying on. As my mom brought glasses of lemonade to us all the doorbell rang.

I stood up to go answer it. Upon opening the door and looking outside, a cascade of bullets rained down, covering our porch in a hail of gunfire.

Gina dropped her glass and came running. My dad, Mr. Palmer, and Mr. Richardson all took their wives to the ground and covered them. Devin tried to hold Delila, but she had already taken off toward me. All anyone could hear was the sound of Gina screaming my name, "GAB-RI-EEEEEL!" As she and Delila reached the front door, the music stopped...

About the Author

Tre LaVin was born in Fort Worth, Texas and raised in Aurora, Colorado. He is a U.S. Army and Operation Iraqi Freedom Veteran. He is a pastor, husband, father, brother, uncle, and son who is proud to be doing the Lord's work out in the field. He is also the author of his autobiography, *Thank God At Rock Bottom, Jesus Was The Rock That I Hit!* and a poetry collection, titled: *Clutching Bricks: Poetry Without Apologies*. He lives in Humble, Texas.

CPSIA information can be obtained
at www.ICGtesting.com
Printed in the USA
BVHW071701250521
608094BV00003B/403